The
WICKED BAD

Karyn Gerrard

CRIMSON
ROMANCE
F+W Media, Inc.

Crimson Romance
an imprint of F+W Media, Inc.
10151 Carver Road, Suite 200
Blue Ash, Ohio 45242
www.crimsonromance.com

ISBN 10: 1-4405-7346-8
ISBN 13: 978-1-4405-7346-0
eISBN 10: 1-4405-6675-5
eISBN 13: 978-1-4405-6675-2

Printed in the United States of America.

10 9 8 7 6 5 4 3 2 1

This book is available at quantity discounts for bulk purchases.
For information, please call 1-800-289-0963.

Dedication

My thanks to Crimson Romance for accepting this story.
Also, as always, I dedicate this to my live-in hero, who would
not let me give up on this manuscript. A few years and a few
edits later, turns out he was right. There, I said it publicly.
You were right, babe. Love you.

Chapter One

You can't go home again. But what did Nick Crocetti know? He'd never had a home.

One thing he could not stand was any form of rank sentiment. Especially in himself. The emotion had been missing from his tumultuous life for years, so why in hell did it rear its ugly head now?

Nick glared at the name on the colorful flyer he had pulled from under the door of his bar. Veronica Barnes Titus. *Ronnie Barnes.* The annoyingly cheerful flyer announced the grand opening of Titus Bakery on Waterloo Street.

It couldn't be her; she had left town ages ago. Titus? Right, he'd heard talk she'd married, was she still? He hoped the rumors of her recent divorce were true. Any talk of Ronnie Barnes perked his interest through the years, though he would outwardly pretend he didn't give a damn what she'd been up to.

Nick crossed the threshold and closed the door behind him. He tossed his keys on the bar and hit the light switch by the door. Fluorescent lights flickered and buzzed washing the brick interior in a hazy illumination.

He spread the flyer out on the counter and read it again. When he saw her last at her father's funeral, he'd kept a respectable distance. She was still the luscious blonde he remembered and she still wore glasses that always seemed to slide down her nose. It's not as if they'd ever spoken to each other. Nick knew her brother Tyler slightly; at least by sight, they were the same age. He should've walked up to her and offered his condolences, but she no doubt would've seen the blatant lust in his eyes. A crass statement at a funeral, especially her father's.

The memories roared back whether he wanted them to or not. Nick arrived in Rockland, Maryland, in the twelfth grade. At the time, he had nowhere else to go, so he lived with his uncle, a man he barely knew because his parents had washed their hands of him. Nick's home had never been a happy one, and with his parents obtaining a divorce and going their separate ways, neither wanted a hulking six-footer who hadn't finished growing and who had a penchant for getting into constant trouble.

His lips curved into a cynical smile as he thought of his first motorcycle, a fire engine red 1975 Indian. Nick removed the baffle plates from the bike's exhaust muffler just to annoy the hell out of everyone with the noise. The personification of the bad biker dude, he'd been all attitude and presence on his red Indian. He spoke to no one and everyone got out of his way when he walked down the hall at school. Nick hated Rockland High. Talk about not fitting in. He wore black leather even back then.

One person he'd noticed was Ronnie Barnes. Two years younger than him, she'd been outgoing, gregarious, and popular and everything he wasn't. She had a killer body then and from what he observed three years ago at a distance, she still did.

While her glorious curves attracted his attention and stirred his raging teenage hormones, the intense feelings expanded beyond lust the more he'd observed her. Kind and generous with her friends, affectionate and teasing with her brother, she appealed to him in all ways: his first crush. Hell, his first serious bout of puppy love, unrequited though it had been.

Nick leaned on the counter and gazed outside into the parking lot of his small bar, The Chief. There stood the object of his current affection, his 2013 Dark Horse Indian, one of two motorcycles he owned. Damn, the bike was beautiful, all black and sleek with the telltale fringed leather seat. If anyone touched his baby, he would rip out their spine. The bike was parked where he could keep an eye on it while he worked in his bar.

His thoughts drifted back to Ronnie. Nick wasn't afraid of anyone or anything, then or now. However, Ronnie Barnes rendered him mute. For months he tried to screw up the courage to approach her and to talk to her, but by March of his senior year—he was gone.

The bakery was located at 35 Waterloo Street; if he remembered right it used to be a beauty parlor back in the day. Maybe he should check it out.

Suddenly, Nick felt as if he were back in high school. Why did Ronnie Barnes have him acting this way? The unsure teenager he used to be, which he thought he'd moved past. Not as far as she was concerned, apparently.

Over the years, there had been no shortage of women. One of Nick's rules since he lost his virginity at age sixteen was that he never slept with a woman more than once. Cold and calculating perhaps, but it worked so far. Sex to Nick was a necessity of life, like air or food, nothing more. He never once engaged his heart in his many encounters.

When did he last have sex? *Oh yeah.* He smiled knowingly. Four days ago he hooked up with a waitress at the Top Hat Diner. What a night. Is that what he wanted with Ronnie Barnes? A night of hot, wild sex? Swinging from the rafters, pounding, driving with plenty of raw, animal lust? *Hell, yeah.* Nick dreamed about sinking into her luscious body since his teens. He imagined how tight and wet she'd be when he'd finally get her under him. He hardened just thinking about it. His leather pants groaned in protest at his sudden erection. *Down boy.* Nick folded the flyer and stuffed it in his back pocket. Guess he'll be buying cookies or bread in three days' time. He watched as the Budweiser truck pulled into the parking lot to make his delivery. The time had come to get to work and push Ronnie Barnes out of his mind.

*

You can't go home again. These words haunted Veronica Barnes for weeks leading up to her return to her hometown.

She cocked her head and watched as the MacDougall company crane put into place the sign advertising the name of her new business, Titus Bakery. The temptation to call out to the workers that the sign didn't look level nagged at her, but surely these guys knew their business. After some measurements, the men did hang it to her satisfaction.

She scanned the front of the building. Not too large and kind of quaint with the old brick facade. This building had been around since the twenties. The place was hers now, lock, stock, and worn bricks. The ceramic tile by the front entrance looked decades old, but was still in beautiful shape. The large storefront windows were also a big plus. However, sun beating in on baked goods might not be a good idea. She would see about shaded glass or maybe refrigerated units for her cakes. Veronica pulled out her iPod Touch and typed reminders for later.

The unmistakable hum of a V-8 engine came up behind her. It had to be her brother, Tyler. Who else would be driving an obvious unmarked police cruiser? Tyler Barnes opened the door of the black Crown Victoria and leaned on the driver's side window.

"Hey sis, what in hell is this Titus Bakery? You're a Barnes again."

Veronica pushed her glasses up her nose; they had a habit of always slipping down no matter how many times through the years she bought new glasses. She slipped her iPod in her pocket, and then crossed her arms in mock annoyance. Tyler, her older brother by two years, was a detective with the Rockland Police Department. He was blond and at least six-foot-one with a lean musculature a cover model would envy. He always spoke his mind, at least to her.

"I don't like the name Barnes Bakery. Besides, since I'm using the settlement money to start this venture, it seems fitting to call the place after Billy-boy Titus."

William Titus—her fourteen-week mistake. A lesson learned. Hot, feral sex doesn't translate into a lasting love or marriage. She secretly wished it did. Caught up in the throes of a passionate, drunken weekend with rich, real-estate entrepreneur, William Fortesque Titus II, they'd wound up at one of those cheesy Vegas chapels that dot the strip. Thirty-six hours later, they'd realized their mistake.

Now divorced, she'd been given a check with an obscene amount of zeros on it. Sucking up her courage, she quit her consultant's job in San Francisco, California, and headed back home to Rockland, a small blue-collar city nestled on the Chesapeake across from Washington, D.C. Her brother was the only family remaining in town. Her father died three years ago, and her mother moved to Port Ritchie, Florida, to live with her older sister, Elmira, among the orange groves and alligators.

At twenty-nine, Veronica was ready for a little life change. She took a deep breath hoping to inhale some fresh air. Instead, she wrinkled her nose.

"Ewww, is that the pulp mill? It smells as bad as when I left."

Tyler shrugged. "I don't even smell it most days. Besides, it's always worse when it's hot and muggy like this."

This was hot? Tyler should've come out to California for a visit, she thought to herself.

Before she could speak, Tyler sighed at what he knew was Veronica's unasked question. "Yes, I put someone trustworthy on getting the flyers out, slipped under doors, left on car windshields, yadda, yadda." He held up his hand to still her response. "Get that look off your face, I supervised. It was done to your exact directions. Besides, I shouldn't have done it, all as it's actually illegal." He grinned mischievously.

Veronica hugged her brother tight.

"Thank you, I'm so nervous. The mixers and ovens were delivered this morning and Ty, I had no idea the flour's in seventy-five-pound bags! How am I going to lift it?"

Tyler stepped back and placed his hands on her shoulders.

"Are you sure you're ready for the grand opening in three days? Have you even hired any help yet?"

"I can manage for a while until it gets off the ground." she replied.

"You've got the money, Ronnie; hire someone and fast. Damn, you told me with the baking alone you will be up at four in the morning. You can't put in fourteen hour days."

Veronica rolled her eyes. Tyler always ragged her ass since they were kids. But, she grudgingly had to admit the golden-haired Adonis had a point.

"I'll call the employment agency. The reason I called you besides lifting the flour is I want you to inspect the rooms in back. I'll be living there."

Tyler's mouth dropped open. "Why? I said you could stay with me as long as you like. Why live in cramped rooms in back of the bakery? You'll never get away from the heat and the smell."

"There's nothing wrong with the smell of fresh baked goods. In fact, it's been proven no one gets angry in a bakery, the odor soothes people. Plus, they come in to purchase baked goods for happy occasions like birthdays and bar mitzvahs," Veronica laughed. "How can you have your lady friends over if your sister's there? I must be cramping your style at the moment. Of course, there were a few nights you didn't come home."

"I was on a stakeout. I told you," Tyler grumbled. "Now you sound like a wife."

"You know Mom is heartbroken. Last time we spoke she asked if you were seeing anyone serious. She's dying for beautiful blond grandchildren, Ty."

"So, go ahead. Give her some," Tyler snapped.

"I touched a nerve. Sorry, Ty. Come on, let's go in and do an assessment. You can help me finalize my list of what products I'll be selling. I'll be starting with a just a few things, french bread, Parker House rolls—"

"Cinnamon buns?" Tyler's face brightened. "Damn, you make the best cinnamon buns!"

Veronica laughed. She'd missed Tyler. Gone from Rockland, how many years? Wow, almost ten years except for a few visits and the funeral.

She missed her father deeply. How she would've loved to have him here helping, giving advice and hugs. Teagan Barnes had been a strapping, handsome man who hadn't been sick a day in his life until a heart attack took him away. His sudden death devastated them all, especially her mother. Veronica lifted her chin in determination. A new beginning, she was due.

Chapter Two

Veronica sat back in her chair tapping her pen nervously against her cheek. The grand opening was tomorrow and she still hadn't found anyone to hire. After interviewing eight people, she had found none suitable. She didn't want some gum snapping, surly teen, or the older woman who did nothing but complain about her creaking and aching hips. She had one more interview. If they had a pulse they were hired, at least temporarily. She thought people were looking for work with the downturn in the economy. Maybe she was crazy for trying to start a business in this unstable environment. She'd just finished forming that thought when a young woman walked through the door. She stood before Veronica and smiled broadly.

"I'm your eleven A.M."

"You're hired."

The woman laughed. "You don't recognize me, do you?"

Veronica looked down at the application. Julie Denison. She glanced back at the woman, must be about her own age.

"Sorry, no. I haven't lived here for ten years, I'm afraid I'm terrible with faces and even worse with names."

"You once came to my rescue. In high school, Penny Winters was teasing me mercilessly. You stood up to her when no one else would," Julie said quietly.

Of course, Julie had weighed at least two hundred and fifty pounds in high school, no wonder she didn't recognize her. The curvy woman standing in front of her now was a far cry from the morose, overweight teen of their high school years.

"I know I look different. It took a couple of years of hard work, dieting, exercise, and it's a daily damned struggle to keep it off, but I'm doing it."

"Ah, then why work in a bakery? Won't the temptation—you know, cookies and cakes. I'm sorry, I shouldn't have said that. Julie, you look

11

great. I admire the fortitude it took to achieve your goal." Veronica smiled sheepishly.

"Working here will keep me on the straight and narrow, much like an ex-alcoholic working at a bar. Plus, I figured you could use some help. I ran into Tyler downtown two days ago. I'm in between jobs. I need the work, Ronnie."

"As I said, you're hired. I'll be using you to help the customers, watch the inventory, and let me know what's getting low. I'll be doing the baking. Can you start right away, like tomorrow?"

Julie slammed down her purse on the counter. "I can start now."

Veronica nodded. Things were looking up.

*

Grand opening day arrived, and her idea of distributing flyers seemed to have worked as they had a steady stream of customers. Julie handled the customers well, *'Four years working at the Food Lion!'* Already they worked like a well-oiled machine. The cookies were selling like hotcakes, *'little bakery joke'* Veronica laughed to Julie, especially the chocolate chip oatmeal with pecans. Veronica stayed in the back furiously mixing up another six dozen when she glanced at the clock, almost lunchtime. She had to cover Julie's hour break. Glancing in the mirror, the reflection showed a sweaty mess. Her long, wavy hair was tucked haphazardly under a plastic cap with a few loose strands hanging in her face.

Stepping into the bathroom, she washed up, removed the cap, and straightened her hair. Taking off her industrial apron, she strode into the shop. *Five customers, excellent.* Julie reached under the counter for her purse.

"I'm going to Jake Spooner's diner for a chicken salad plate. Can I bring you anything back? I know you won't take a break."

"Actually, a chicken salad plate sounds wonderful. And an iced tea extra-large, no sugar." She pressed a twenty into Julie's hand. "Lunch is on me today. You sit and enjoy your break."

"Thanks, boss. Oh, down to two dozen cloverleaf rolls, they're a big seller."

Veronica nodded. "I'll be sure to make more tomorrow. Go to lunch."

Julie waved as she walked out the door. Veronica exhaled and then glanced around the store.

Her own business. Her own bakery. How long had she dreamed of this? Since her teens when she found she could whip up bread and rolls better than her Granny Jennie. There was nothing like running your hands through the dough, kneading and creating. She received more satisfaction in one day with her own bakery than she did all eight years at Byant Consulting. Yes, it would be hard work, but she reveled in it.

After ringing up an order, Veronica heard the door bang open. She glanced quickly and observed someone wearing motorcycle boots marking up her newly varnished and polished wood floors. What was that knuckle dragger doing in her bakery? She had to wait on someone else and never got a chance to look much beyond the scuffed boots, but she could hear the big ape lurching about her bakery. He clomped about the place. Her face flushed in annoyance. The man couldn't stand still. He walked from one end of the bakery to the other. She had the feeling he stole glances at her, but every time she looked up all she could see was his broad shouldered back.

Veronica hoped the biker would make his selection quick and get the hell out of her place. Not the type of customer she wished to have.

*

Nick's restless gaze moved toward Ronnie Barnes. Damn, she appeared more beautiful than his heated, lascivious dreams had conjured. He felt like a smitten teenaged fool, which he chalked up to lingering hormones, but now he wondered. However, his heart was firmly folded in a lockbox under his bed and that's where it would damn well stay.

His thoughts wandered as he stared at the bread display. Nick loved all things classic whether it was fine wines, imported beers, or classic rock from the sixties and seventies. He also loved the classic figure on a woman. Curves—something to hold on to. He couldn't abide those skinny twigs with their collar bones sticking out. He hated holding a woman close, his hand trailing down her back and all he could feel was her spine. Nick liked a little meat on the bone, and loved to hold a handful of plump, succulent breast. Even in high school, Ronnie filled his ideal of the perfect figure. Standing at five-foot-six, she was tall enough to wrap those shapely legs around his waist as he slid his hands over that fantastic ass and pumped into her against the bakery wall. Great, he stood in a bakery with a raging hard-on. His obvious erection would be enough to scare the old women. He should've worn his jacket, but it was too hot out. His cock ached and throbbed. The leather pants hid nothing. He was determined he'd talk to her today even if it killed him, and at this rate it would.

He glanced down at a display of whole wheat rolls. *What do I know or care about fresh, friggin' bread?* He breathed deeply. He had to admit it smelled good. All of it.

"Can I help you?" The soft, feminine voice asked.

The voice had an edge, like his presence annoyed her. He held his breath and turned to face her.

*

Veronica gasped. This man was the furthest thing from a knuckle-dragging Neanderthal. She glanced up, he was so—tall. He had to be four or five inches over six feet. His skin had a dusky, golden color. His amber eyes glittered with a shade of gold that couldn't be real. His hair was dark golden-brown with highlights of different subtle shades of auburn. Not too long, but not too short, layered, thick and glorious and it curled at the nape of his neck.

A tiger. He reminded her of a tiger with the eyes and his coloring. He had the sleekness and the power.

He sported a closely-cropped goatee, a darker brown than his hair with flecks of gold mixed in. The man was handsome with a breathtaking ruggedness mixed in. Even William Titus hadn't been this blatantly male. This guy oozed virility and sensual confidence.

Her gaze could not stop from moving downward. He wore a tight black sleeveless t-shirt, which hugged every muscled, ripped plane. Black leather pants caressed his muscular thighs and—her head snapped back up—he had a package that could win a first place blue ribbon on one of those bulge websites, not that she ever visited them. Veronica shook her head to clear away such silly thoughts and forced herself to look at his face again. Why did he look so familiar?

A trace of heat traveled though her as she stared at him. Veronica observed his eyes darken, with interest? Surely, she was mistaken. She licked her lips as they had gone dry, but not her thighs; arousal gripped her tight. She placed her hands behind her and clasped them tightly for they'd started to shake.

"Hi," he murmured huskily.

Oh, god. Of course he would have the deep, let's-go-to-bed, crushed velvet voice to go with the killer, sinful body and face. Dressed as a biker of all things.

"I knew you in high school, well, knew *of* you—" he said.

Her eyes widened in recognition. Veronica was lousy with names and faces, but not his. *Nick Crocetti.* She remembered Nick stood around the hallways at Rockland High, muscular arms crossed with a surly look on his face. He'd never spoken to anyone that she could recall. They didn't have any classes together as he was in the program for the gear heads. Oh, yikes, how terrible, but it was what the people in the vocational courses were referred to. Back then she'd noticed him, how could you not? He'd been big and imposing with a presence you could hardly ignore. He still did. He filled her store with his obvious masculinity. This man was a walking sex bomb.

"Nick Crocetti?" she questioned softly.

He seemed genuinely surprised she remembered him.

"Yeah, and you're Veronica Barnes. Hi."

Her throat closed over. Never in her life did she have such an immediate reaction to a man like this. All she wanted to do was throw him to the floor and crawl all over his tall, muscled frame. Taste his golden skin. Kiss those full lips. Grind her very core into him. Her face flushed hot.

"Are—are you here to buy some of my baked goods?"

Nick reached out and gently brushed something off her cheek with his thumb. She gasped. The slight touch seemed to affect him as it did her, for his hand trembled briefly.

"Flour," he said so quietly she could barely hear him.

"Married?" he mumbled in a louder voice.

"Divorced," she replied. "Some quickie, Vegas mistake."

"This Saturday night ..." he began, his voice sounded a little stronger now.

"Yes?"

Veronica gazed up at him, a wave of hopeful anticipation rolled through her. Surprising.

"Well, I thought maybe—you and I—go out. Saturday night. Or not."

"Go out where?"

Damn, it was like they were back in high school.

"We could go out to dinner. Or a movie. You call it." Nick smiled.

God, his smile could light up the Eastern Seaboard there was so much wattage behind it. She glanced outside, spying his bike.

"Okay, dinner it is, and how about a nice, long ride on your motorcycle? I've never been on one."

"Cool. I'll pick you here at seven o'clock."

He turned quickly and walked toward the door. Nick glared at Jake Spooner, who was on his way in carrying a foil take-out plate and a drink. Nick didn't hold the door for him, just barreled out toward his bike. Perhaps she imagined it, but the look he gave Jake seemed territorial, as if he dared the man to make a move on her. A low, animal snarl escaped his lips as he strode outside. His growl sent a wave of heat straight between Veronica's legs. She watched attentively as Nick climbed on his bike. He turned and looked back at them standing by the window and his eyes narrowed as he gave Jake one last dangerous stare. Nick turned the ignition, hit the kickstarter, and roared off.

Her hands were shaking. A date with Nick Crocetti. Back in school the girls all used to giggle, sigh, and admire his form from a distance. They even took bets on who'd walk up and speak to him, but ultimately they'd all chickened out. Nick had that imposing and dangerous look that would appeal to teenage girls in spades. Hell, it appealed now. After the upright, uptight, Armani-suit-wearing William Titus, this would certainly be going the opposite end of the spectrum. Why did she agree to go out with him? Though, thinking back, William Titus turned out to be a tiger in bed. Why did she get the feeling Nick Crocetti could out-tiger William Titus in all ways? Sexy beast in bed and out of it, she imagined.

She snapped back to attention when she heard Jake Spooner clearing his throat. He smiled and held up a foil-covered plate and a drink.

"Your lunch, free delivery!"

Veronica took the food from him and placed it on the counter.

"Thanks, Jake. You didn't have to deliver it. Julie could've brought it back."

Jake had been in every day since she'd started renovating. He wasn't bad looking as such, but she really wasn't interested in him in any way—not even as a friend.

Jake inclined his head toward the now empty parking lot. Her store was quiet for the first time all day. Figures, Jake would never leave now.

"Was that Nick Crocetti?"

Veronica took a long, satisfying slurp of iced tea.

"Yes, we went to the same high school."

"He owns a sleazy biker bar down by the docks, The Chief. He named it after a motorcycle," Jake sneered. "He's a thug, did time in prison. He deals drugs in his bar. You can't be considering going out with him."

Veronica halted in mid-slurp. Prison? Drugs? She let blind lust allow her to say yes to Nick, the leather-clad biker hunk. An ex-convict who deals drugs. She groaned inwardly.

Does she dare ask her cop brother about Nick Crocetti? Should she cancel the date? She didn't even know how to get in contact with Nick unless she dropped by his bar. She glanced at Jake. The man looked a little too smug about the gossip he just unloaded.

"He did ask. I'm thinking about it," she lied smoothly.

An older woman walked through the door.

"Sorry, Jake. "I have to go assist this lady. Thanks again for bringing me my lunch!" She dismissed him brightly.

*

During a brief lull in customer traffic later that afternoon, Veronica asked, "Julie, do you know Nick Crocetti at all or anything about him? Do you remember him from school?"

Julie's eyebrow rose. "What made you bring him up?"

"He was in here today while you were on lunch. What have you heard?"

Julie shrugged. "I know he owns a biker bar or whatever it is. Why, if you don't mind me asking?"

Veronica tapped the counter nervously. "He asked me out on a date this Saturday night."

"What?" Julie yelled. More quietly she said, "The Terminator asked you out on a date?"

"What is he, an assassin? Why is he called the Terminator?"

Julie laughed. "Actually, that's my name for him. Remember Arnold Schwarzenegger in *Terminator 2*? The black leather and the big-ass Indian motorcycle? Or did Arnold ride a Harley in the movie?" Julie shook her head and continued. "Anyway, Nick is way yummier looking than Arnold. I saw him once in the parking lot of his bar washing his bike with his shirt off. I nearly drove off the road. Gorgeous body. I think he lives above his bar." Julie sighed deeply, as if picturing a shirtless Nick in her mind. "I've never spoken to him and you're hard-pressed to find anyone who has. I'm shocked. He came in here bold as brass and asked you out? Wow."

"What about the rumors, Jake said …"

Julie waved her hand dismissively. "Jake is jealous. I don't put any stock in those rumors, why not ask Tyler? He'd know if Nick is some drug-dealing scum."

Veronica laughed. "Tell Tyler? I wouldn't dare. He'd have Nick brought into the interrogation room and then beat the snot out of him with a phone book. I'll find out for myself. Nick Crocetti doesn't intimidate me."

Right. There wasn't much in this world that rattled her, but standing before the sexy presence of Terminator Nick rocked her senses. Her body sparked and thrummed with such sensual awareness just thinking of him. What would the actual date be like?

Chapter Three

Nick hadn't slept for two nights. He had restless-sheet-twisting-brain-racing-staring-at-the-clock-with-cat-naps-in-between type of sleep. Where to take Ronnie for dinner? Where to go for the drive? What in hell would they talk about?

What surprised him more than anything in their brief, disjointed conversation was the fact she knew him. He'd no idea. How did she know of him? He had to admit he was damned curious. Also, he was secretly and smugly pleased.

Sitting up straight in bed, he bent one leg and rested his arm on his knee. The rising sun filtered through his blinds and the rays spread across the carpet. He had to decide where the date was tonight. Maybe up to Easton on the Ocean Gateway, it wasn't far. They had a great seafood restaurant. After, they could go to a piece of secluded beach he knew of.

The restaurant wasn't too fancy, though there was that upscale wine bar he liked. *Perhaps another time.* His eyebrow arched. Another time? Planning on a second date already? *No.* His one and only date with Ronnie Barnes would be tonight. The time to fulfill his fantasies at long last was—tonight. A quick toss in the sand should satisfy all his sexual cravings, past and present. He imagined them rolling around in the pounding surf, with him pounding into her. Jesus, his cock twitched and hardened at the thought. He hadn't been this damned aroused in ages.

Nick groaned. He forgot to buy something at her store. He left in such a hurry. He made a quick exit in case she changed her mind. Well, that and his hard-on. The one he had now felt worse. Christ, he *was* still in high school. How many mornings did he wake up in this condition thanks to his Ronnie Barnes fantasies? He had to get her out of his system once and for all.

Nick threw back the sheet, time to get moving. He had to make sure his employee, Kevin Conway, would be covering him tonight at the bar.

*

Veronica closed at six o'clock on a Saturday night. Before she even bought the place she decided she wouldn't be open Sundays. She needed one day off at least. She also decided she wouldn't open until noon on Mondays giving her another morning she didn't have to get up at three-thirty. She glanced at the clock on the wall. Close to seven and Nick would be here any minute.

She'd spent the last hour showering, waxing, plucking, and anything else she could think of to make herself look presentable. The decision on whether to wear her hair pulled back or leave it down plagued her for hours. The final decision was to leave her hair down. Using a curling iron, she made soft tendrils to frame her face. How much makeup? She wasn't one to slather it on with a trowel, but she did like to wear a little. Veronica decided a little powder and a slight bit of rose blush and matching lipstick was all she needed. Now, to choose her outfit. She could go full-bore slut mode, but she didn't really own any sexy clothes. Well, except for one dress William made her buy in Vegas. The outfit was cut so low her size D-cups spilled out into her lap. Turn suddenly and her nipples would pop out and wink at someone. No way.

If she would be riding on the back of a motorcycle, then she wouldn't wear a dress that would inflate like some slutty umbrella. She chuckled to herself at the image. Choosing a new pair of jeans and a pink V-neck sweater, not cut too low, but enough to give a peek of cleavage, she dressed quickly. The outfit she selected fit in all the right places giving her a younger and perky look even with her bust size. She sighed, always had a full bust. In high school boys were always trying to cop a feel to see if they were real, or try and prove she shoved a whole box of Kleenex down her front. William used to go on and on about it, forever grabbing her like he married her tits instead of her.

*"I William Forteque Titus the II, take these tits to be my legally married
… "* Veronica giggled. Even his name—'Tit-us.' It fit. If you can't laugh
about it, why bother?

She glanced at the wall clock above the door again. She grabbed a
foam container and with long handled tongs picked out the two best
cinnamon buns left on display and placed them inside. Nick left in such
a hurry the other day she never had a chance to offer him anything.

She heard it, the deep, throaty growl of a large displacement motorcycle
pulling into her parking lot. He was prompt. The anticipation built all
day. Really, she hadn't dated or been with a man since she and William
parted fourteen weeks after the marriage from hell. Hard to believe that
had been close to eight months ago.

Her mouth dropped open as Nick walk toward her door. She expected
him to be in his leather, kick-ass biker gear. He wasn't. Nick wore tight-
fitting black jeans, expensive ones from what she could see, and black
cowboy boots. He also wore a brown muscle-embracing sweater, a light-
weight blend that accentuated his golden coloring and stunning upper
torso to best advantage. The sleeves ended just past his elbow giving a
lovely view of muscled forearms dusted with golden-brown hair. Oh my,
he looked as sweet, sinful, and delectable as her cinnamon buns.

She unlocked the door and he smiled. Nick had gorgeous, straight
white teeth that looked even more brilliant against his dusky skin.

"Hi Nick, come in for a minute."

He glanced at his watch. The gold watch looked like one her father
used to wear, one you had to wind. It wasn't new and didn't look cheap.

"Only for a minute, I've a reservation for us in Easton."

"Easton, I haven't been there in years! We used to all go to the
Waterfowl Festival every year when we were kids—don't laugh. They
had rides, food, music, and crafts. It was a lot of fun."

She sighed happily at the memories. Snapping back to the present,
she held out the foam container to Nick.

"Something for you, to prove I can actually bake. You left in such a hurry the other day I didn't get a chance to give you a free sample."

*

Nick opened the container. The fresh odor of cinnamon and sugar invaded his nostrils. Damn, it did smell good.

She stepped closer. Her breasts brushed by his arm sending a wave of heat all through him. He almost dropped the container.

"I use cream cheese icing. The trick is not to overdo it and use just enough to meld with the cinnamon."

He closed the container. "They look really good, thank you. We'd better go."

"Did you want to leave them here and get them on the way back?"

Nick mulled it over. Was it an invitation to come back to her place? Wishful damned thinking.

"I can put them in the basket on the back of my bike."

He strode to the door and held it open with one arm. His other hand still gripped the container.

She walked past him, close enough to brush by his sweater and allowing him to have a whiff of her delicious aroma. Some fruity body wash, delicate, not overpowering. He could detect expensive cologne mixed with her distinct, sexy, feminine scent. He closed his eyes briefly and savored it. Nick stepped aside so she could lock the door.

Walking side by side toward his bike, Ronnie cocked her head. She seemed to do it a lot and he thought the gesture cute.

"This is a different motorcycle from the one you had the other day."

"Yeah, the Dark Horse is only a one-seater. This is an Indian FE. Lots of room for two."

"A picnic basket, Nick?"

He shrugged nonchalantly. "I have a few things in it." He shoved the cinnamon buns in the basket, then handed her a helmet. "We'd better get going."

Thirty minutes later and they were sitting in the restaurant. They enjoyed a bowl of crab chowder and were waiting for the steaks to arrive. In between courses they made small talk about generalities, nothing too heavy or probing personally. Nick was too preoccupied by the perpetual hard-on he had since Ronnie climbed on the back of his bike and snuggled her lush body against his. The sensation of those luscious breasts slammed against his back with her small, delicate hands around his waist, and her feminine core nestled against his ass—lingered. Nick had felt her heartbeat, every intake of her breath, and he could feel it still. Never was he so in-tune with a woman's body before, every twitch and every movement without sex being involved. His cock was as hard as granite. Unbelievable. The erection felt damned painful and embarrassing.

"Nick?"

The steaks arrived and he missed what she'd said. *Idiot.*

"Sorry, Veronica. Guess I'm a little tired. It's been a long week, must've been for you as well with your grand opening."

"Nick, you can call me Ronnie, most people do. I guess I'm tired too, but it's a good tired. I never knew there was such satisfaction in owning your own business and being your own boss. But you know what I'm talking about don't you, Nick? How long have you had the bar?"

She smiled sweetly at him while she cut a small piece of her medium-rare steak and popped it in her mouth. Damn. Even watching her eat affected him. He imagined that sexy mouth on his dick. His cock jolted in response. It had a life of its own and he couldn't control it.

The point she made was a good one. He liked being his own boss. Granted, he wasn't making a huge profit, but living upstairs saved him from renting an apartment elsewhere and let him indulge in some of his hobbies. He had developed a few.

His thoughts drifted back in time while they ate. Years back, after eating another Kentucky Fried Chicken snack box for an umpteenth meal, Nick decided he wanted something more out of his life than greasy take-out. So he began to read, voraciously devouring books on all manner of subjects. He loved wine and was quite knowledgeable on the different regions and vintages and collected rare bottles. The wine he ordered tonight reflected that. Szekszardi Bikaver, a Hungarian red he knew would go perfectly with their steaks. Nick's thoughts snapped back to the present.

"I bought the property about nine years ago when I came back to town. It didn't cost much, considering where it was located. I paid cash for most of it and only needed a small loan. My uncle backed me for the difference. The place is all mine. You're right, there is a certain satisfaction in owning your own business. But it does take up a lot of time and energy. I have one employee and he covers me if I need time off and helps around the place. It's not very big."

These words were the most he'd said to her or anyone lately.

"But it's yours, Nick. No one can take that away from you," she whispered. She raised her wineglass. "Here's to us and our businesses, may they flourish and bring us the success we want." Nick smiled and clinked glasses with her, they both took a sip. "Oh, Nick. The wine tastes great with the steak, full-bodied and lush."

Like you, he almost said aloud. He wanted to taste her, every damned inch of her skin. Savor her like a fine wine. His cock jerked again. He had to get rid of this madness, this crazy lust, and it had to be tonight. Maybe he could talk Ronnie out of dessert.

*

When they stood to leave, Veronica impulsively slipped her arm through his. She felt him stiffen. Was her touch so horrible? She gazed up at him and his face seemed to be devoid of emotion as it had been since they'd became reacquainted.

Nick surprised her tonight so far. The ease in which he ordered the wine, his mode of dress, and when she had managed to get him to talk it was obvious he wasn't a knuckle-dragging nimrod. He fascinated her to no end. The questions she wished to ask mounted, but Nick remained guarded about a lot of things, his past most of all. This would require a good deal of patience. Veronica could be patient when needed. Instead of being put off by his reaction to her touch, she pulled herself closer to him. Did he just moan? The sound so soft she'd barely heard it. She smiled. Perhaps he was not as unaffected as she thought.

The time was close to nine o'clock when they arrived at a small piece of beach not far outside of Easton. Nick removed a blanket and the basket from the back of the bike.

"Don't get any ideas about me. I saw it in a movie once, I'm no romantic," he said.

Veronica had to admit, she was having a nice time. She enjoyed sitting behind him on his bike as he raced up the highway. Her arms clung to his broad, muscular back and chest. Feeling the powerful bike vibrate under her and feeling Nick vibrate next to her was a total turn-on. Touching and holding on to him sent such waves of pure, raw heat through her body. Though at first, she was scared to death. Before they left, Nick instructed her on how to be a passenger. Lean into the turns when he did and don't clutch him too tightly. Veronica knew she shamelessly felt him all over as he drove. Nothing prepared her for the rush of excitement, not only being curled against all that male muscle, but the feeling of driving fast on the open road with the wind whipping around her body. She wished she could've taken the helmet off and let the wind take her hair skyward. The sensation was incredible, a real rush.

She followed him toward the beach. The shoreline wasn't very big, but private, as you couldn't see the road or much else from their vantage point. Wonder how many other women he brought here, she thought cynically.

He spread the blanket and assisted her in sitting down. Again, the touch of his hand made her face flush as well as parts further south. Nick sat next to her with one leg bent and he rested his arm on the top of his knee. They sat quietly and gazed out over the water. The waves caressed the sand with a serene almost hypnotic sound.

"I saw you talking to that wuss, Jake Spooner, as I left the other day. I can imagine what he said about me," Nick said in a voice so soft, she hardly recognized it as his.

Veronica cleared her throat uncomfortably.

Nick laughed. "I see. Go on, amuse me, what did he say?"

"Um, he said you were in prison—" she began.

"Jail. Not prison," he retorted.

"There's a difference?"

"You've got the cop for a brother, you tell me," Nick snapped. He shook his head, more gently he said, "Sorry. It's a touchy subject. City jail, for assault and destruction of property. Prison usually means a state or federal beef. Mine was local and a long time ago. I did my time and it's over. I don't like talking about it."

"He called you a thug and said you deal drugs among other things." She shouldn't be telling him this, but the words tumbled out of her.

"Really? And still you went out with me? Are you some thrill seeker, one of those good girls eager to rub up against some wicked bad? Is that why you're here? I'll be as bad as you want, just say the word."

His voice grew tight and edgy. Barely restrained anger simmered below the surface, she could hear it.

"I'm just telling you what Jake said, you asked."

Nick stared at her for several moments. "Yeah. I did. Sorry. I haven't been out on a date in awhile."

"You haven't been with any women…"

"Oh, I didn't say I haven't been with women, just haven't been on a date." The right corner of his mouth twitched in what Veronica supposed was amusement.

Veronica laughed out loud, she couldn't help it. Nick smiled broadly in return. He could be funny. How wonderful.

He opened the basket and lifted out a couple of candles. Reaching in his pocket for a lighter, he lit them and buried the large pillars in the sand.

"No breeze tonight, perfect." Next, he brought out a bottle of wine and two glasses. "A Riesling, hope you don't mind a little more wine."

Veronica couldn't believe this. She watched as he skillfully removed the cork and poured the wine in the crystal U-shaped goblets. Nick handed the glass to her. Reaching in the basket again he came out with a rose, the most perfect red rose she'd ever seen. He handed the flower to her.

"For you."

Chapter Four

Veronica wanted to cry. Literally bawl her eyes out. There wasn't a long list of men she'd dated. Besides William Titus, she'd only slept with three other men, only dated two of them seriously. None of them did anything like this. Not even close. Veronica brought the flower to her nose and sniffed, the rose smelled glorious. She glanced at Nick framed in the moonlight. As he sat and watched her, she couldn't help but compare him to a Roman god. The temptation to throw her arms around his neck and kiss him senseless was potent. Not romantic. *Right.*

"Thank you, Nick," she whispered softly.

She had to fight the tears from collecting in her eyes. Beautiful man, beautiful gesture.

The mood changed as they drank the wine, they became more relaxed. Nick opened up a little more. He volunteered there were drugs around his place, but he didn't deal them. He had a rule: not in his bar. Outside in the parking lot was their business. He admitted to smoking weed now and again. When in his early twenties, he tried more hardcore drugs though he didn't volunteer which ones and she didn't ask. Nick seemed to like she didn't pry.

Veronica found herself fascinated by this man. The statement he made about her being a thrill seeker still resonated. Did she want to rub up against the wicked bad? Nick had grown quiet. She saw those amber eyes of his darken. He was going to kiss her.

He lifted her chin with his knuckles. Nick leaned in and brushed his lips softly against hers. The feather-like touch seared and sizzled. A deep rumble came from Nick's chest. The sound started from his toes and shook his whole body. Out of the corner of his mouth snarled a sexy, animal groan of pure longing.

Before she knew it, Nick pulled her on top of him. He lay back on the blanket. Veronica could feel every hardened edge of him. Nick was aroused, how could she miss it? He grabbed either side of her head and held her still while he plundered her mouth. Nick tasted every inch and his tongue worked magic and ignited the simmering flame within. She had never ever been kissed like this.

*

Nick couldn't hold back any longer. She tasted of a delightful mixture of wine, sugar, and cinnamon. Her tongue met his at last, enthusiastically meeting his thrust. He was ready to go off like a roman candle. With Ronnie, he wanted to go slow. Why, he wasn't sure. He was never known for taking things at a deliberate pace with any woman. *Slam, bam, thank you ma'am,* had pretty much been his credo since his teens. There were times he could be considerate and see to a woman's needs. He just made damn sure he saw to his first.

His hands moved downward and gripped her luscious ass and he brought her in tight against his throbbing cock. She gasped briefly, but then ground her hips into his aching prick. Ronnie pulled away, sat up, and straddled his hips. She continued to move hers in a slow, sensual grinding motion. Ronnie's eyes were closed. He grabbed her hips and thrust upward. Sex without the penetration. Nick watched her expression; she hid nothing. Christ, she was going to come right here just by rubbing against him. Her head dropped back and she cried out and shuddered. Ronnie's whole body trembled in release. Nick almost spilled himself in his jeans right then and there. Never saw anything so sensual as Ronnie climaxing merely by rubbing against him. He sat up and kept her firmly straddling his erection. If it was hard before, now it was beyond: damned cement.

In a deft movement, he removed her sweater and tossed it to the blanket beside them. Damn, her breasts. This woman did not need extra padding or one of those push-up jobs. He laid soft kisses across the top of her cleavage then cupped one of her breasts. A handful and then some, for Nick didn't have small hands. Squeezing gently, his thumb flicked the already hardened nipple. He reached and pulled the strap down off her shoulder and the breast popped free. Nick lowered his head and captured the nipple in his mouth, laving, licking, and sucking. He pulled the nipple gently with his teeth. Ronnie groaned and squirmed, which set him on fire.

"Ronnie," he rasped. "Don't—don't move so much, I'm losing control ..."

"I can't help it!" she cried.

Ronnie lowered her other strap, and released the other breast. She held them both up to him as if she were offering them as a gift or a delectable dessert.

"Suck them hard—please."

That did it. The barely concealed control he hung from disappeared. He climaxed right there spilling himself as a randy teenage boy. Christ, how embarrassing. He had never done it before. He'd never been whipped into such a sexual frenzy without actually having sex. He twitched and shuddered as his cock continued to spurt his release.

She knew.

Nick couldn't look at her. He bit his lip to try to keep from moaning, but it was no use. His whole body trembled from the intensity of his release. Ronnie had secured her breasts back in her bra. She still sat astride him and hadn't moved. Cupping his cheeks, she forced him to look at her.

"Nick," she said softly.

She kissed him, tenderly and with a slow gentleness that took his breath away. His cock hardened again, he wasn't finished. Ronnie no doubt felt his hardening prick because a smile curled about her lips as she kissed him.

"That was intense for both of us," she whispered. "I wonder what sex itself will be like?"

He couldn't. As much as he wanted to take her right now and grind her into the soft sand, he couldn't. Nick was a damned mess, emotionally and physically. In all his many sex encounters, nothing had been this intense or all-encompassing. He felt out of control and he didn't like it. The notion of seducing her caused his dick to throb. She was more than willing. Every fantasy he ever had could be realized, and then he could take her home and move on with his life.

However, Nick realized having sex would only percolate his interest more. He didn't want to go down that road. Dating, sex with one woman and engaging his unused heart.

"I didn't bring condoms with me." *You liar.* He had two in his wallet and more in the storage box of his bike. He kissed her again. "Guess we'll just have to make out."

Wouldn't this just stoke his fire more? The truth was he didn't want to leave yet. Even though embarrassment seeped from every pore, he wanted to stay. Kiss her. Hold her. Talk about confused. Nick rolled her under him and she squealed and then laughed. He rolled her again, off the blanket and into the sand and kissed her, deeply and thoroughly.

"Oh Nick," she breathed, her voice sexy and husky.

It went on, for how long, Nick had no idea. He never kissed a woman like this. This resembled a scene out of an old movie, *From Here to Eternity* with Burt Lancaster and Deborah Kerr rolling around in the sand and surf. Nick also loved classic movies.

"Nick!" Ronnie squealed. "The tide's coming in and we're getting wet!"

He smiled wickedly. "It's only a little water. Won't hurt us, unless sugar, you melt in water? Better tell me now."

*

"No. I don't melt."

Well, that wasn't quite true, she melted in his arms. The best make-out session she ever had. Nick could kiss. Veronica kissed him with everything she had, which caused her glasses to steam up. She rubbed herself against him again—against *the wicked bad.*

A low, languid moan escaped from Nick. The noise rumbled up from his toes and shook him. Let the tide come in and drown them, as long as she was here—with him. Veronica reached under his sweater as her hands explored and roamed all over his taut body. His muscles bunched and flexed at her touch. Her hand met the crisp hair on his chest and she ran her fingers through it.

"Off," she snarled as she pulled at his sweater.

Nick grabbed her hands, stilling them.

"We'd better not." He glanced at his watch. "It's past midnight. We still have a half-hour drive back to Rockland yet."

Flustered, she rolled away, and with trembling legs stood and reached for her sweater. Nick stood behind her and rested his hands on her shoulders. He leaned down and kissed the nape of her neck. Moving her hair, he began to lay hot, searing kisses on her shoulder and down her arm.

"I'd better stop or we'll be watching the sun rise."

Why this turned into the hottest make-out session in her life was a puzzle. Veronica moved away from him and pulled her sweater over her head. She leaned down and reverently picked up the rose.

"Thank you, Nick. For this, for everything."

He smiled briefly, quickly gathered up the wine, glasses, candles, and shoved them in the basket. "You're welcome."

They didn't speak the whole way back to Rockland. He walked her to the door of her bakery. Taking her hand, he laid a brief kiss on it.

"Thanks, Ronnie."

Nick sprinted down the steps without another word, and without looking back climbed on his bike and roared off into the night.

Chapter Five

Two in the morning, and Nick stood in the shower. The ice cold water pounded his body and pounded the part of him that wouldn't calm the hell down. He even took care of it as soon as he walked in the door, but he just stayed hard. Nick leaned against the tile with one hand, the shower head pointed straight at his unruly, hard cock. Maybe he should call that 1-800 number, *if you've had an erection for more than four hours*—but he wasn't taking any of those prick pills. Twenty-five years from now, who knows? He smiled wryly. It was obvious he didn't need them now. How in hell could he sleep in this condition?

More importantly, why back away from Ronnie's obvious invitation to explore every part of her body? He wanted all of that, didn't he? To bury himself into her softness right to the hilt, pound away until she was wiped away from his dreams and desires. What must she think of him? Coming in his jeans and trembling in her arms like a damned fifteen-year-old boy. Then, dropping her on her doorstep and run off like a thief in the night without a word or if he would even call her. Nick had no idea if he would call her again, not if he was going to react like this. He slammed the water off in disgust and reached down to fist his stiff-as-a-pike cock, his hand moved up and down the length.

Here we go again.

*

Across town, Veronica lay in bed, wide awake in her darkened room reliving what happened the last few hours. They'd rolled around on the beach and made out like a couple of horny teenagers. Was that it? They were trying to relive and recreate an obvious secret attraction—from high school? Veronica reached for her iPod Touch and placed the buds in her ears and selected her rock music folder. She turned it down low, Creed's *Overcome* growled in her ears. "Completely stunned and numb" pretty much described how she felt.

Nick Crocetti was nothing like she imagined. He was a man she could fall in love with, but Veronica wouldn't make that blunder again, mistaking lust and a physical spark beyond all reason for any kind of long lasting emotion or relationship. The stunning fact remained: she climaxed by rubbing against him. Never had she done that before.

Veronica felt her cheeks flush. She knew she wasn't a Frigidaire babe. The few times she had sex she was an active and enthusiastic participant. William Titus showed her a few things and she wanted to explore it with Nick, in every way and in every position. If anyone could give her multiple orgasms, it would be Nick.

She rolled over and looked at her pewter lighthouse clock on the bedside table. The time read two in the morning. She would give him a few days, then what? Call him? Stalk him? Send him sexy emails or texts? More cinnamon buns?

A lone tear escaped her eye. William Titus had hurt her. Veronica thought she was in love, deeply and completely. After the drunken sex fog lifted, it had become apparent he didn't feel the same. Her heart still ached by being rejected that way. William Titus couldn't run away fast or far enough. She cried on and off for days.

Never again. All she wanted from Nick Crocetti was that glorious body of his, nothing more, and damn it, she was going to make sure she got it. The drought ended now.

Veronica's eyes closed briefly, her thoughts raced. Was Nick embarrassed because he shot off too soon, in his jeans no less? No condoms? She didn't buy that for a minute, him?

By his own admission he had plenty of women. She must ask Julie what she'd heard about Nick prowling around since he returned to Rockland. And jail. He became upset talking about it. Again, so much she didn't know. What about his parents? All he mentioned was an uncle and not with any warmth.

In between songs she heard her phone ring. She scrambled out of bed almost getting caught up in the tangle of sheets.

"Hello?"

"Veronica Barnes? This is Doctor Callum Murphy at Rockland General. Your brother asked me to call you. He's all right, but he was wounded tonight. Tyler took a bullet to the shoulder and he wants you to come down right away."

Veronica's hands began to shake, Tyler shot—oh, dear god.

*

It was ten o'clock Sunday morning and Veronica hadn't slept. She stayed with Tyler as he would be held overnight for observation. She had to return home and catch a nap before going back for the evening visiting hours.

Only a flesh wound, Tyler assured her. He wouldn't tell her how he came to be shot. Stupid police business. Tyler made her promise not to call their mother in Florida, she would rush back and there was no need as he would be released Monday. Veronica was inclined to agree, their mother didn't need this right now. She made a mental note to exclude this incident from their next weekly phone conversation.

Veronica pulled in behind the bakery and parked her five-year-old Mustang. She walked around the corner and gasped. Leaning against the front brick facade with one leg up against the wall with his arms folded, stood Nick.

She stopped dead in her tracks. She felt strange and flustered. He must have heard about a cop being shot and found out it was her brother, Tyler.

"How's your brother, Ronnie?"

Her lower lip began to quiver. Nick pulled her into his close embrace. There was nothing sexual about his touch. He stroked her hair as she sniffled noisily.

"I was so scared, Nick."

"I know, baby," he whispered.

"You came over here to see if I was okay?" she asked, her voice slightly muffled from her head lying against his chest.

"Well, to tell the truth, I came over for more cinnamon buns."

He cupped her face and gazed at her. His eyes twinkled teasingly, but Veronica also glimpsed a warmth she'd had not seen before. He studied her as if he were committing every freckle to memory. He leaned down and kissed her nose. Her glasses slid down and hit his lips. He smiled and gently pushed them back.

"Really? Cinnamon buns, you—you enjoyed them?"

"Almost as much as I enjoyed you. They almost tasted as sweet," he whispered.

Veronica gazed up at him. He smiled the most devastating, sexy, wicked smile she'd ever seen. *No, don't. Don't fall for him. Don't you dare do it. I just know he'll hurt me.*

He kissed her, not the searing, flames-on-high kiss of last night. This was the most gentle, caring kiss she'd ever received. Affection, warmth, and kindness. Tenderness.

"Do you want to come in?"

Nick leaned his forehead against hers. "You look exhausted. You need sleep more than anything. I'll call you in a couple of days."

"Really, Nick? You'll call? You're not just saying that?"

Oh shit, I sound needy and desperate, the last thing I want to do. Chase him away why don't you!

He backed away, his thumb still caressing her cheek.

"I'll call. Have half-dozen cinnamon buns set aside for me."

He strode to his Indian and climbed on. Nick turned the ignition, hit the kickstarter, and roared off down Waterloo Street.

She stuck the key in the door and opened it, still in a trance from his kiss and embrace. That's what she wanted, for someone to give a damn.

Forever. She had this sick feeling it would never happen to her. Nick was only interested in her cinnamon buns.

"Well, it's a start," she chuckled.

Veronica tossed her small purse on the counter. First, she would sleep. Then she would call Julie once she was more lucid. Julie would have to cover her tomorrow while she saw Tyler settled. She was going to insist he stay with her at the bakery for a couple of days. Veronica could hear him balk now. Next on her to-do list—baking. Cookies, bread, rolls.

Locking the door, she sauntered off to the back rooms. Her living area wasn't bad. There was a good size living room and bedroom. A tiny kitchenette, but with the full bakery kitchen to use, she didn't need anything larger. The unpacked boxes sat in the corner, not that she brought a lot with her. Veronica sold everything in California except a few books, DVDs, and clothes. Didn't even have a set of dishes yet, just borrowed odds and ends from Tyler.

The bathroom was cramped with old fixtures, but kept in good repair. Thankfully, the previous owner had air conditioning installed front and back. The place stayed cool even when all the ovens were going full tilt. Entering the bedroom, she peeled off her clothes and crawled into bed. Exhaustion caused her body to shake, or was it Nick's tender kisses and rapt, gentle attention? She was touched by his concern. Nick Crocetti—cared.

*

Veronica had called it. Tyler did nothing but complain all the way to the bakery when she picked him up Monday morning from the hospital. Turning left on City Road heading toward Waterloo Street, she glanced at her brother sitting in the passenger seat.

"You're staying with me at least two nights, Tyler, get used to it."

"You have an ancient twenty-inch TV. No cable, no dish," he grumbled.

"I haven't had time to get anything installed since I opened," she snapped. "There, something for you to do. See about getting me the best deal possible, cable, satellite, doesn't matter. That should keep you occupied. Besides, I have a DVD player. Hook that up and watch movies, I have a box of them."

"Probably chick flicks," he sulked.

She glanced at him again. "Come on Ty, you know what movies I like. I have *The Guns of Navarone*," she teased. "And the special edition set of *The Omen*, and *The Boys from Brazil*. You can have a Gregory Peck film festival and I'll supply the popcorn. I'll make your favorite cookies to boot."

Tyler smiled. "If only I could find a woman like you, sis, I'd marry her in a heartbeat."

Veronica laughed. She really missed being with Tyler all these years, the closeness and the teasing. They always got along even when they were kids. By the time they had reached their teens, they were the best of friends, even hung out together in high school. She glanced over at her drop-dead, handsome brother. Why hadn't he found someone yet, was he even trying? Unlucky in love—the both of them. That fact was surprising, since their parents fell in love in their early twenties and married. Their mother and father were deliriously happy up until her father died. She and Tyler had great role models for happiness, love, and marriage, then why at thirty-one and twenty-nine were they still unattached?

She thought again of Nick stopping by to check on her. What man did that after only one date? Veronica couldn't stop thinking about the heavy make-out session on the beach. Her lips were still raw and swollen from his passionate kisses. Her face and breasts stung gloriously from his closely cropped goatee rubbing against her skin. She wanted to feel that silky, soft facial hair rub against the inside of her thighs and that magical, probing tongue of his firmly planted in the deepest and wettest part of her. Veronica had to bite back a moan from escaping her lips from the image. What would Tyler think of her and Nick Crocetti? She was hesitant to bring his name up and find something out about Nick she really didn't want to know. She didn't want her brother trying to dissuade her.

What did she want with Nick? She wanted sex. No two ways about it, she ached, and damn it, she should've dropped to her knees in the sand and begged.

Flipping her blinker on to turn onto Waterloo Street, she made a promise to herself. Next time she was alone with Nick Crocetti she would jump his fine, big bones.

Veronica didn't have to wait long. After getting Tyler settled in and the DVD player hooked up, she prepared the smelly nacho chips he liked. It took all afternoon for her to make the arrangements, but Tyler sat happily surrounded by fresh baked peanut butter cookies and a six-pack of Miller MGD. When she heard the opening rousing score of *The Guns of Navarone*, Veronica sauntered out front to do a quick inventory. Thanks to a quick nap in between baking the cookies and making the nachos that afternoon, she wasn't as tired as she had been earlier. She looked at the wall clock. Close to nine o'clock. Enough time to watch a movie with Ty, and then catch a little more sleep before she had to do the baking.

Veronica bent over to grab her clipboard when she glanced outside. What she saw made her drop it on the floor with a clatter.

Under the streetlight with his long muscular legs spread apart and his hands at his side clenched into fists, stood Nick Crocetti. Getting past the initial shock of seeing him, what shocked her further was the look on his face: Pure, feral, animal lust. Want. Desire.

Chapter Six

Veronica's hand clasped her throat. The usually cool, detached Nick showed every emotion he no doubt felt. He wore leather pants again, but this time they were brown and he wore a gold leather jacket with no shirt underneath. She caught a tempting glimpse of perfectly formed pecs and knotted, muscled, flat abdomen all dusted with the same shade of golden-brown hair on his head.

Nick strode toward the glass door. There was no mistaking his purpose in being there. The reason clearly showed on his face and the erection he didn't hide also decided proof. One hand unclenched and he ran it down the front of his pants as if to bring her attention to it, as if she could miss that. He looked as if he was about to break the glass to get to her, like that movie with William Hurt, *Body Heat*. Only she wasn't some sultry Kathleen Turner in a low cut blouse and tight skirt. She wore a pair of baggy sweatpants and an equally baggy Baltimore Orioles t-shirt. His gaze was hot and hungry; he looked as if he wanted to devour her.

His hand continued to stroke the front of his pants and his eyes closed. Her mouth lost all moisture. Nick didn't seem to care if anyone saw him. His golden-brown eyes snapped open and he gave her the most raw, sexy gaze she'd ever seen. He began to look around the front entrance. Veronica grabbed the key under her counter before Nick did pick up a planter and sent it careening through the glass door or window. Try explaining that to the State Farm guy. *Yeah, a man did it to get at me so he could ravish my body.* Somehow, Veronica guessed that wouldn't be covered in her insurance policy.

Nick stepped through the door and reached for her face with both hands, kissing her deeply before she even had a chance to speak. She melted against him. He took her hand and placed it over his hard-as-a-rock dick. Veronica moaned, she couldn't help herself. He had a brick down his pants, surely.

"I've been in this condition since Saturday night," he rasped.

His hand lay atop hers, pressing and urging her to grab as much of him as she could. She did. Nick groaned right from his toes.

"Is your brother here?"

Damn, how could she have hot, wild, feral sex if her brother was in the next room?

"We—we can go to your place."

"I won't make it," he gasped. "Is there somewhere we can go? I want you, Ronnie."

Oh yeah. Now. Her mind raced. Where? Obviously not in front of the store windows like they were in the red light district of Amsterdam. She grabbed his hand.

"Out back," She looked up at him. "Did you bring …"

He nodded. "Oh, yeah."

Veronica pulled him out through the front door, locked it behind her, and ran to the back of the building. She could hear Nick's boots right behind her. Was she insane? Yes, insane with lust. She led him to a secluded alcove hidden from the alley and parking lot. No one would see them. Nick arched an eyebrow.

"Outside? Won't the neighbors hear? Your brother?"

It appealed to him what she proposed; she could see the approval in his glittering, amber eyes.

"I haven't any neighbors. The businesses are closed and Ty is watching *The Guns of Navarone* on full tilt, he won't hear a thing."

"I like old movies, but this isn't the time to discuss them." His eyes darkened.

"Nick, I want you, too. Do it, now. Hard and fast. Against the wall, bent over those crates, I don't care."

Veronica could not believe she said those words. Never in her life had she spoken so plainly, so wantonly. The conflicting sensations of being on fire, but soaking wet, rolled through her. She trembled and shuddered with anticipation, her body heavy with need.

"Please." She reached out and laid her hand on his bare chest. His heart thundered under her touch. Nick removed his jacket and dropped it to the ground.

"Hard and fast, coming up, baby. I couldn't go slow right now if I tried."

Veronica lowered her sweatpants and smiled seductively. The long t-shirt barely covered her rear.

*

Nick gazed at her intently, her face alive with emotion. Ronnie wanted him almost as much as he wanted her. Never in his life, in all his many sexual escapades with women, had he been whipped into a sexual frenzy like this. He had to have her—or die. The sensation was that dire and serious. These feelings and emotions drove him to ride by her bakery constantly the last twenty-four hours. He was ready to break the damned glass to get at her, the urge and the need that strong. What in hell was wrong with him? Reaching for her waist, he lifted her t-shirt. Oh, sweet Christ, she didn't have any underwear on.

His cock slammed against his zipper. He plundered her mouth at the same time he cupped her curls and one long finger entering her folds. Ronnie was as wet and ready as he could hope for. She gasped under his lips. It wouldn't take much to make her come, could he wait? He moved in and out while his tongue matched the thrusts in perfect unison. She rode his finger; he felt the hardened nub and rubbed as her feminine softness clutched his finger and held on. Ronnie came in less than a minute. Nick swallowed her screams as he kissed her even more deeply. Finally, her shuddering stopped. Reaching in his back pocket, he pulled out a condom.

"Yes, Nick," she whispered.

Nick looked around, how to do this? He sat her on the tall crate. Perfect. Exact height he hoped for. All he had to do was stand in front of her, spread those luscious thighs, and take what he had dreamed about since he was eighteen. He lowered his zipper. He wore no underwear either tonight. Grabbing his hardened cock, he pulled it out.

Ronnie's eyes widened. The look of amazement on her face caused him to smile. She reached out and her fingertip followed the pulsating vein from the base to the tip. He bit on his lip so that a barely restrained hiss emitted from his lips.

"Nick. Your cock is so—thick," she whispered, almost with awe.

"Help me out here, Ronnie." Anything to get her to touch him.

Ronnie didn't hesitate. She grabbed him with both hands while he rolled the condom over his rock-hard prick. He was so rigid; he had never been this stiff before. His breath puffed out in ragged gasps, he'd be hyperventilating soon. Yeah, that would be attractive. Breathe into a paper bag while having sex. His hands grasped her shapely legs and he pushed in, just a little bit to let her get used to him. Ronnie gasped and moaned all in the same breath. He pushed in a little more.

"Hard and fast, Nick."

He lost control. The thread snapped and he pumped her with wild abandon. He cupped her ass and brought her closer so she took all of him, right to the hilt.

He closed his eyes. If he thought Ronnie was in another orbit the other night, she couldn't have been in the same dimension as him at the moment. Pure, unfettered pleasure, the most intense sex he'd ever had. Nick had plenty of sex since he was sixteen years old. So many women he'd lost count.

Her inner muscles clenched and grasped him and he moaned. She joined his groans of pleasure and the sounds made him move faster. Ronnie shuddered, her back arched as she came, again and again, waves of it. Nick joined her as every muscle in his neck clenched. He literally roared with the release, an animal sound he'd never heard come from his own lips before. His eyes opened and he glanced down at Ronnie. She smiled. He withdrew, his cock still semi-erect. The astonishing thing was his body was ready to go again. Right away.

Ronnie stood on her toes, took his flushed face in her hands, and kissed him, hard. He clasped his hands around her waist and pulled her against him and kissed her back. The deep, passionate kiss stoked the already roaring flame between them. The air was heavy with the musky odor of sex.

Ronnie tore her lips away and walked over to the wall, her hips swayed suggestively. Facing the wall with one hand flat against the brick, she leaned over and gave Nick a peek of paradise as her t-shirt rode up. She rotated her hips in a slow, sensual tease.

"Hard and fast, Nick. Again," she said huskily.

Nick's jaw literally dropped open. Another fantasy of his about to be fulfilled, taking her from behind. Reaching down, he tore off the used condom and fumbled in his pocket for another. He took the used rubber, the wrappers, and shoved them in his coat pocket. Sheathed, he walked up behind her, moved her shirt up, and explored the round, tight globes of her luscious ass. He stroked her wet pussy. Never in his fevered dreams had he imagined Ronnie to be this passionate and eager. He loved it.

Hard and fast? Whatever the lady wished. Holding her steady, he spread his large hands on either side of her thighs and plunged in deep, right to the hilt. Nick pulled out his cock, and then thrust. She laid both hands flat against the wall again.

"Deeper, Nick," she moaned.

God, how could he get any deeper? The thrusts and the slow withdraw continued and her moans grew louder. He found a slow, languid pace that they both rode. Nick could've done this all night. The air around them was heavy and desirous. The sounds of skin making contact and the sucking, wet sound of her feminine core stoked his lust higher. He thought it the most glorious sounds in the world. Minutes passed, and still he continued the pace. He quickened the tempo as her inner muscles clenched his cock tight in an intimate embrace. He thrust faster, Ronnie cried out his name. He loved the sound of his name on her lips as she came.

Nick's intense and numbing climax came right after hers. His knees were ready to buckle. He pulled out, tore off the condom, adjusted himself, and zipped his pants. Nick couldn't handle anymore tonight, even though his body screamed for more. But it wasn't just his body, his emotions were in turmoil. Intense sure, but this was more than just sex and it confused him. He didn't want to feel anything for her. He fulfilled enough of his fantasies regarding Ronnie Barnes. He should get on his bike and ride off. Move on with his life—without her in it. He didn't want to care for her or anyone.

Ronnie walked into his arms and kissed his chin affectionately, her fingers stroked his goatee. Nick stood stock-still, not moving or reacting to her tender kisses. He didn't dare, or he would take her back to his place and make love to her as she deserved to be made love to. In his bed all night—with an aching, tender passion. Not this animal sex out behind her bakery. Even though it was the most satisfying off-the-charts animal sex he'd ever experienced.

Nick glanced down into her beautiful, shimmering, blue-gray eyes. Ronnie looked at him with such warmth and pleasure. If he was a total jerk he would just turn and walk away. He'd done it before with other women—many times.

His legs wouldn't move. What does he say to her? Some glib, offhand remark dismissing what they shared? Was she as deeply affected as him? Gazing into her eyes, he could see her emotions were in chaos the same as his. It seemed Ronnie didn't hide her feelings. Unlike him, he thought cynically. Nick already wore that mask of indifference he'd worn his whole life. The mask became harder to wear with Ronnie Barnes.

*

Veronica's heart fluttered madly in her chest. She had to protect herself before she fell off the cliff into a pit of tumultuous emotions. William Titus was still too painful and raw. The scab had not even begun to form over the open wound.

Hot sex does not translate into a long lasting relationship. Or love. Her hands slowly traveled up his chest, the muscles flexed and bunched under her touch. How she wished it did. Nick grabbed her wrists and gently pulled her away from him.

"I have to go," he said, his voice gravelly and deeper than usual.

He brought her clenched fists to his lips and brushed a quick kiss over them. Nick let go and stepped back.

She had to say something, but what? The unruffled, cool look on his face spoke volumes.

"Nick, I want something from you, but it's not what you think. I'm not looking for anything serious here. I want us to continue this—sex. I liked it, a lot. I want more. That's all I want from you."

Veronica watched him closely. He didn't react or blink his eyes, nothing.

"Sex, baby? No problem." His voice sounded detached and distant. "I can deliver. So, when do you want it next? Should we make a firm time and place? Once a week? Twice? Just tell me and I'll pencil you in."

"You pick the time, I'll be there. I'll even bring the condoms," she retorted in the same cool, detached voice he used.

One eyebrow shot up, did the corner of his mouth quirk slightly? It was hard to tell in the shadow of the alcove. She leaned down, picked up her sweatpants, and stepped into them. She reached for his jacket and handed it to him.

"Thanks, Nick."

He took the jacket and slipped it on. "Fine, I'll get back to you."

She nodded curtly. "You do that, I'll see if I can pencil *you* in."

Nick walked away and didn't look back. In the distance, she heard the familiar roar of his motorcycle as he accelerated down the street.

Hot, miserable tears clustered in the corner of her eyes. This was too much. *He* was too much. Veronica wasn't ready for this. Did she really think she could keep herself removed from him, coolly enjoy his body, then walk away and not engage her heart? Because never had she enjoyed a man or enjoyed sex more than she did with Nick. There was still so much more to explore. Nick may be in her blood, but she would make damned sure he never reached her heart. No man would ever hurt her again.

*

Nick didn't turn toward the dock area or his bar. Instead, he raced through downtown letting the cool evening breeze ruffle his hair. He had to get away from her as fast as he could and he didn't even take the few minutes to put his helmet on. He would let the damn cops stop him, he didn't care. Nick made the turn toward the I-95 north exit. He'd had nights like this before, drive all night to forget. Tonight, he wanted to forget her. Maybe he'd head east and cross the state line into Delaware and head to the Atlantic Ocean to Bethany Beach, a place he favored in the past.

Forget it all. The hurt and the rejection. All these years nothing had changed. *I want you for sex.*

Apparently that's all he was good for. Man meat. Stud on speed-dial. Order him up like he was a damned pepperoni pizza. He should cut it clean.

Forget her and her delectable curves, her hot, luscious mouth, and her inviting, moist core that clenched him tighter than any woman ever had before. Her sexy demands that he go deeper, harder—faster.

His first instincts were right. Nick never should've had sex with her. He wanted more, just as he suspected. The more he had sex with Ronnie, the closer she'd worm her way into his heart. Nick inhaled deeply. He could smell her essence all over him. He would never get that scent out of his nostrils as long as he lived.

Chapter Seven

The early morning going-to-work flurry of customers had thinned out, and it was too early for the lunch crowd. Veronica had been open a week now, and couldn't be more pleased at the results. A lot of the traffic she reasoned was due to the fact of the newness of the bakery. She knew the novelty would wear off after a couple of weeks, but the whole experience had turned out to be enjoyable.

If only she was able to get enough sleep. She tried to watch the rest of the movie with Tyler last night, but couldn't concentrate. Mumbling she was tired, Veronica retired to her room, but tossed and turned and watched the clock move. At three in the morning, she rose and began the ritual of preparing the dough for her bread and rolls.

Nick. Her mind raced and relived everything that happened. How did it fall apart? Veronica tried to be affectionate with him after they were done, but he just stood there like a marble statue, his face devoid of feeling or emotion. The only thing she could do in response was slam up her protective fence as well.

It all went downhill from there. They were both frosty and detached treating what they shared as if it had been nothing at all. How could it turn so cold and meaningless to him? The sex was the best she'd ever had. If she continued with Nick, it would get even better and go right off the charts. Even though the sex had been wild, there was so much more underneath, she didn't imagine that. Veronica wouldn't let her emotions come into play here, since it was obvious Nick didn't. How to explain the romantic gesture at the beach? No doubt all part of the seduction and probably one he used many times with countless women. Veronica slammed her apron on her baking table and headed out front where Julie did a count of the bread and rolls.

"Take a break, Julie." Veronica pulled the stool to the counter and motioned for Julie to take the other one. "I wonder if I can ask you about Nick Crocetti."

Julie placed the clipboard on the counter and sat on the nearby stool. "I don't know what I can tell you."

"Tell me about the women. I take it there have been a lot of them."

Julie exhaled. "You'd better put the kettle on."

Veronica laughed nervously. "Shit, that doesn't sound good."

"I'll have a cup of tea with milk and a little Splenda." Julie called after her.

Five minutes later, Veronica emerged with two steaming mugs of Twinings English Breakfast Tea. Sliding it over to Julie, she sat again.

"Okay, spill."

"I've heard talk, 'love 'em and leave 'em, Nick'. I heard he'd slept with Miss McGregor."

Julie lifted the mug and took a sip.

Veronica cocked her head. "Miss McGregor, the history teacher?"

"Think back twelve years ago. She was in her early twenties and used to wear those leather skirts split up the back right to her ass, along with the tight sweaters. She had every teenage boy lusting after her."

Veronica shook her head. "Are you telling me she slept with horny teenage boys, Nick included? Isn't that a felony?"

"That's the rumor. I mean really, Nick never looked like a teenage boy, did he? That's the only student I heard about. Nick in the twelfth grade was full grown in more ways than one. So I heard." Julie shrugged taking another sip of tea. "Remember Darlene Cummings?"

Veronica searched her memory and then nodded. "She got around."

"Well, I was in her gym class. I heard her bragging to a bunch of girls in the locker room about Nick and his impressive equipment and his stamina. It's something I've heard many times through the years, from numerous sources."

A sharp stab of jealousy slid in under Veronica's ribs. Turns out, she was just one in a long line starting with a damned schoolteacher in a slutty, leather skirt.

"Nick dropped out in March, did you ever hear why?"

Nick told her jail, but she wanted to hear what Julie knew. Julie, who it seemed, was a fountain of information.

"Yes, I heard he was in prison somewhere upstate, robbery or some such. Then I heard after he was released he took off and disappeared. When he showed back up in town four years ago, I admit I was shocked, thought he dropped off the edge of the map." Julie related in a confiding tone. "I take it he didn't tell you anything on your date."

"No. He made it quite clear he didn't want to talk about it, I didn't press," Veronica wasn't going to tell Julie it was jail for assault. She wanted to keep Nick's confidence. "What about his uncle?"

Julie took another sip. "Henry McCann. He died last year. Cancer."

"Oh," Veronica exclaimed softly. "He never said. But I got the impression they weren't close."

Julie crossed her legs. "Back to the women. Who knows what's true. I only know the man doesn't talk to anyone and as for the women he's been with, it was of a brief and intense duration and it was always him that walked away. A lot of broken hearts I would imagine. Is that what he did with you?"

Veronica was taken aback. "What? No. At least, I don't think so. I think we'll be seeing each other again." But now, she had her doubts.

"You had sex with him, didn't you?" Julie whispered. "Don't deny it, I see it on your face, you're blushing. Is it true, the equipment and the stamina?"

"Julie," she said in a warning tone. "I can't talk about it."

"I'll take that as a yes. Wow. Nick is walking testosterone. I'm impressed and maybe just a tad jealous." Julie teased gently.

"What about the drugs?"

Julie inclined her head to the back rooms. "Why not ask your Viking god of a brother? He must be up by now. He could tell you. Personally, I haven't heard much. His bar's in a rough part of town."

"I can't talk to Tyler about this, not yet," Veronica laughed. "Viking god—Tyler?"

"Don't worry, I'm not interested, not that he would even look twice at me anyway. Talk about Nick getting around, your brother's no slouch." Julie giggled.

"Oh? You've gossip on my brother? Now it's your turn to spill! And what do you mean he wouldn't look at you twice?" She demanded.

"I'm not gossiping about Tyler with him in the next room. Look at me, Ronnie. I might pass as borderline cute, if that. I've been called plain by members of my own family and they love me. I know my limitations. Tyler likes beauty. That's all I've seen him with, though not lately. Your brother and I are friends, nothing more."

The bell tingled over the door as a woman and a young girl walked in. Julie put down her mug. "I'll go help this lady."

Veronica sat, stunned. She learned quite a bit, even about her brother. She'd been away from home too long. It seems her *close* brother kept things from her. What made her insides roil and lurch was the talk about Nick. She should've guessed. *Love 'em and leave 'em Nick.* Great. Is that what she really wanted? No strings attached—casual, hot sex? She thought so. Nick was—complicated. She got that already after one date. He knew what he was doing, the restaurant, not too expensive and not too cheap. The beach, the candles, the wine—and the rose. *The rose.* She would've happily fallen at his feet with that gesture. The big, tough biker was a romantic at heart when it suited him. Nick could've easily had sex with her on the beach, he had seduced her thoroughly and completely, and she would've done anything. Instead, he held back.

Then to be waiting at her door to comfort her about Tyler, the tender way he held her and kissed her. It took her breath away. Showing up at her door the next night in that state, like he would explode if he didn't have her was sexy as hell. That alone sent her over the edge, never had she been so—horny. A man wanted her that much. It was appealing, enticing, and downright satisfying.

Who was the real Nick? He obviously wanted her to believe he was all those men rolled together: romantic, tender, wild, and dangerous. Veronica thought they'd connected somehow, that something happened between them. This was her downfall, she read too much into sex. Not this time, that is if Nick ever called again.

Veronica took a sip of tea and looked at the phone. Would he call? Should she call? She shook her head and headed out back. *High school, they were in damned high school.*

*

Across town, Nick arrived back at his bar. He did head into Delaware and drove straight to the ocean. The night passed quietly as he sat on the beach and watched the sunrise. He'd called his employee Kevin on his cell and told him to open. Nick hung around Bethany Beach and had an early breakfast. He did a lot of thinking. Lunch rolled around so he had a coffee and sandwich at the Kool Bean, and then decided to head back. Now mid-afternoon, he told Kevin to take a break, he would cover. Not many in the bar this time of day, a few barflies or the unemployed, probably laid off from the pulp mill. Nick inhaled, he should've showered first before coming in to work, but he supposed he smelled no worse than the guys propping up the bar. Maybe he wasn't that anxious to wash off Ronnie's essence.

Nick picked up a few empties from the tables. What possessed him to go to Ronnie's place like that? He must be obsessed. He wanted more. He wanted her. It would be breaking his own private covenant; he never slept with a woman more than once. Nick stood up straight.

Except one time. Darla McGregor, schoolteacher. He closed his eyes. Damn. The woman was only four years older than him at the time, as she was a new teacher fresh out of college. Darla reached out to Nick innately sensing his self-imposed isolation and loneliness. She invited him to her apartment for dinner. He never should've gone, but he did. Someone paid attention and took the trouble to talk to him. He wound up in her bed more than once. Only the second woman he'd ever been with. He had been eighteen at the time of their affair, legally an adult. He thought he knew what he was doing.

Yeah, right.

Nick's eyes snapped opened and he placed the empties in the crate by the back door. He thought he was in love. Darla showed him things and made him feel—damn. As if she could ever be serious about a troubled kid desperate for love. Pathetic really. Nick made a vow after Darla dropped him that he'd never let his heart be engaged with any woman ever again. His emotions were all over the place at eighteen. When Darla told him it was over, he rode off into the night to points northward, Cowentown in fact. He stopped at a biker bar outside the town limits, got drunk, and started a fight. The bar had been trashed. What was the end result of his emotional meltdown? He was thrown in jail and his damned uncle wouldn't bail him out.

It will teach you a lesson, boy. His Uncle Henry sneered. Left him to rot for six months. Nick never returned to Rockland High. Sitting in jail for a long stretch will do things to you. Nick swore no one would let him down again. He locked his heart up tight and threw away the key.

His thoughts were interrupted by a slim man of medium height walking through the door. Nick glanced at the stranger. The man had long, black hair to his shoulders and crisscross scars on his cheek. What caught his attention were the eyes. They were dead—like a doll's eyes. He sized him up immediately. He didn't like the look of him at all.

Nick stood behind the bar. "What can I get you?"

The man glared at Nick, his face stern and resolute. "Got any Kilkenny?"

Nick curled his lip. *Irish accent.* Rockland was a blue-collar city with a deep, Irish background and roots. You only had to drive around the small city and see the names of the streets, Erin, Orange, Patrick, to know the origins of the founding fathers. Four decades ago families brought over their paddy relatives to work either at the pulp mill or the now empty sugar refinery not far from Nick's bar. Not so much anymore. Wonder where this Mick came from? Nick was half-Irish himself, on his mother's side of the family, but he didn't brag about it. The uncle that left him in jail was his mother's older brother. Mean bastard.

"American only, dude. Pick your poison," Nick snapped.

"Give me a Budweiser."

He turned to get a bottle from the refrigerator behind him and reached for a frosted glass. By the time he turned back, the Irish guy was deep in conversation with a couple of Nick's customers and showing them little packets of white powder. Nick's fury boiled.

"You. Irish. Over there," he barked, pointing to the other side of the bar.

Nick strode over and stretched to his full six-foot-four-inch height. He stood close to the Irishman and glared down at him.

"Listen to me, you Irish bastard. No one sells drugs in my place. You want to sell it out in the alley? Fine. But not in *my* place. Or I will give you a new scar on that ass-wipe face of yours."

The skinny Irish didn't blink nor speak. A slow, smug smile curved on his thin lips.

"Go drink your beer." Nick snarled.

The nearby jukebox played Grand Funk Railroad's *We're an American Band.*

"Your music sucks, mate." The man sneered.

"My music, my place. My rules. So either drink your beer or get the hell out." Nick growled through his clenched teeth.

"Take your lousy American beer and feck off, mate."

*

Ronan McCarthy strode outside slamming the door behind him. He looked back at the bar, *lousy biker scum.* He pulled out his package of Camels and dangled a cigarette from his lips while reaching for his Zippo in his other pocket. Flicking the cover open, he spun the wheel until the fluid lit. Lowering his cigarette into the flame, he inhaled, and then grimaced. *Bloody American cigarettes, as bad as their damned watery beer and their feckin' music.* The flavor was not helped by the acrid taste of the burnt fluid.

Ronan turned and looked at the nondescript building that housed the bar. He was renting a few rooms not far away from this bar. Being smart, he had asked around and heard a hulking biker ran it. Thought it would be a good place to unload a little blow. Should have known, once he stepped inside, he realized the bar was not his type of place.

He watched the biker moving about the bar, collecting empties and talking to customers. He expelled a long curl of gray smoke through his nostrils, his eyes narrowed in annoyance.

Ronan did not tolerate being spoken too that way. *No one* spoke to him that way. He would've gutted that biker like a fish from the North Sea if there hadn't been witnesses. He marked the biker down in his book. He knew who he was, Nick Crocetti. *In my book.*

Chapter Eight

Veronica lay in bed reading when the phone rang. Would it be Tyler? He was back at his apartment and ready to return to work tomorrow, did something happen? She scrambled out of bed and ran for the phone.

"Hello?"

"You weren't asleep, were you?"

Nick. He called. The thrill that shot down her spine made her want to jump up and down with pure glee.

"No, just reading. How are you, Nick?"

"I've been better. I wondered if I could come by and pick you up. It was a slow night and I closed the bar early."

"You need sex?" she replied. As soon as she said the words, she regretted it. The silence on the other end of the line said plenty. "I didn't mean that the way it sounded, I'm sorry," she whispered.

"I want to show you where I live and work. Maybe we could talk."

There was that voice, the tight, barely constrained anger she heard the night on the beach when they touched on his past.

"Come by, Nick. I'll wait out front."

Nick grunted an affirmative and hung up, didn't even say good-bye. God, how stupid could she be? Veronica slapped herself on the forehead a couple of times. *Stupid, stupid.* Really, she wandered about in a forest here, couldn't even see the trees. How to handle this thing with Nick, whatever it was? Maybe she wasn't going about this the right way. Veronica wanted William Titus, she got him, and he hurt her. Did she go and curl up in a ball? No—Okay, for a few days—but she picked herself up and dusted herself off and moved forward, determined she wouldn't be hurt again. Veronica rummaged through her drawers to find something clean and presentable.

Fifteen minutes later, Nick pulled up in front of her bakery. Without speaking, he handed her a helmet. Veronica climbed on the back of his bike and tucked herself close to his body. She laid her head on his back as best she could with the helmet on, and his body tightened at her touch. She affected him and she derived satisfaction from that bit of knowledge. Inhaling deeply, her senses could detect the aroma of expensive, sexy aftershave, leather, and a scent that was Nick's alone. The scent was enticing and male—wildness—a feral tiger. Her crotch nestled firmly against his muscular ass. The friction from the bumps and lurches and the rhythmic vibrations of the bike as he drove caused a landslide of heat to envelope her. The bike and Nick were one entity, each an extension of the other. Dominant, throbbing, and lustful. Desire pierced her. She barely bit off a moan before it floated past her lips.

"Did you say something, Ronnie?" Nick asked above the roar of the Indian FE.

She sighed and let the cool evening breeze knock a little sense into her.

"Nothing," she mumbled in his leather jacket.

Her hands idly caressed the tight, black t-shirt he wore. His body was beautiful, what she'd seen of it. She wanted to lie back on a bed with hands folded behind her head and watch him undress. Veronica shuddered with lust at the thought. She pulled herself closer to him. Nick took her hand and placed it on his heart. She felt his heart beat wildly. The staccato pounding almost matched hers. He moved his hand back to the handle bar of the motorcycle as he turned a corner.

Veronica left her hand there and caressed his chest. His heart was strong, wild, and thumping like mad. She could have sat back here curled around his solid frame all night. The heat he radiated was enough to bake her bread. His nearness certainly raised her temperature. She closed her eyes. He felt so right, so unyielding, and rock-hard.

The motorcycle had stopped; they had arrived at his bar. Veronica blinked slowly as if coming out of a trance. Removing the helmet, she had a look around. His bar was housed in a small building, all red brick, probably the age of her bakery or a little older. It sat in what must've been decades ago a busy industrial area, the sugar refinery and the bottling plant, both now closed, had once employed hundreds. The only industry left in this area was the dock and that stood a shadow of its former self only employing seasonal workers or part-timers. The pulp mill was still in operation, but they were continuously cutting back, who read newspapers anymore?

Times were tough, but Nick must be making a comfortable living. Veronica glanced up. He had a neon sign that looked kind of retro and cool. It blinked *The Chief* in a brilliant white. It suited the aged brick. Old wrought iron steps lead to the front door, which was an ornate carved heavy oak that must've been original to the place. The door had many gouges and dents and every one had a story, she imagined. She headed toward the entrance, but Nick touched her arm to stop her.

"We'll go around back."

Nick took her hand in his oversized one. It was large, warm, comforting, and dry. In the distance a siren wailed mournfully, a common occurrence in this part of the city. Veronica could also hear the screech of an alley cat. Unlocking the door, they stepped into an alcove. A set of narrow stairs hugged the wall on the left.

"That goes to my place. I'll show you later."

Still holding her hand, he flicked the light switches and the bar became illuminated in a soft incandesce. Veronica gasped. Nick's bar wasn't what she expected. The walls were the same brick façade as the exterior giving it a warm feeling like they stood inside a cozy fireplace.

The bar counter looked clean and beautiful with original, gleaming oak containing carved inlayed leaves and nuts that a long ago artisan must have lovingly handcrafted. Veronica ran her hand along the top. It had been varnished many times, but seemed to be in good shape. A few stools sat in front of the bar. There were fourteen small tables and chairs in the place. Over in the corner stood a huge pool table with the same inlayed leaves and nuts design on the legs and trim that were on the bar. The felt was a royal blue color. On the wall hung a rack of pool cues along with numerous framed shots of Indian motorcycles through the decades. The floor squeaked as she walked across the boards. Veronica glanced down, ancient dark-wood plank floor that had seen better days, but clean and kept varnished.

She glanced at Nick standing by the door. He watched her closely for her reaction.

She smiled. "It's lovely, Nick. You can see the care you take. Your personality is in these walls."

Veronica headed to the illuminated jukebox. At first glance she thought it was one of those old ones that still played records, but she observed it played CDs. The retro look fit in with the place perfectly. She scanned down the list of music, all old stuff from the sixties and seventies. Nick walked up behind her and laid his hands on her shoulders.

"All my own choices. If I have to work in here, I'm going to listen to the music I like the best."

His voice sounded soft, but had a powerful purr. Nick was obviously pleased with her positive reaction to his place. Veronica tried not to tremble at the feel of those masculine hands on her shoulders. His warm breath caressed her cheek as he spoke. She inhaled and bit back a moan from his closeness.

"Most of this music came out before you were born," she observed.

"True enough. Take a seat. I'll bring you over a drink."

Nick pushed a few buttons on the jukebox, adjusted the volume, and moved behind the bar. Veronica exhaled and took a seat by the window. She listened to the song, it sounded familiar, no doubt from the sixties.

Nick brought over a Miller Lite and sat it in front of her. He took a seat opposite, twisted the cap off his beer and then inclined his head toward the jukebox.

"The Grass Roots, 1967. *Let's Live for Today.*"

Veronica took a sip. The beer was very cold—perfect.

"Did you choose that song for a reason, Nick?"

"Maybe. It has a good message. One I try to live by. I don't worry about tomorrow. Take the most from living; and take pleasure while I can, why not? I was never a long-term planner, I never will be. I'll never be the white picket fence, sedan in the driveway guy." He took a long swig of his Miller MGD. "It'll never be me. I can't change who I am."

"No one is asking you to change, Nick."

"Most women will try, invariably."

"Have many tried with you?" she asked sweetly.

"A few, I don't give them the chance."

"Ah." Veronica responded sadly. This confirmed what she surmised about him. She took another drink. "Love 'em and leave 'em Nick." More loudly she said, "Don't say a few, Nick. I've heard there've been many, many women."

Nick's eyebrow arched. "Have you? Maybe there has, so what? Does that make you want to run out into the night screaming? I'll tell you this, of all those many, many women I've never brought any of them here to my place, my private sanctuary. You're the first."

Her insides turned to warm lava. The first? Somehow, that thrilled her more than she thought it would.

"Then show me your sanctuary, Nick. Show me your private place," she whispered with emotion.

Nick picked up their bottles. He turned off the jukebox, and then reached out for her hand.

"Then, come."

Veronica followed behind him as he walked through the bar. Nick stopped and hit the light switches with his elbow like he'd no doubt done many times before. She smiled at his automatic action. Up the narrow stairs, Nick let go of her hand, reached in his back pocket for his keys, and unlocked the steel door. Flicking on the light, he placed their bottles on the table near the door.

The living room was huge, maybe two rooms converted into one. Recessed pot lighting dotted the perimeter of the ceiling. In the center of the cathedral ceiling two fans with pewter accents and frosted glass shades provided a slight breeze. Along one wall stood shelving that held hundreds of record albums, CDs, DVDs and other media.

Along the other wall was stereo equipment. She walked along the wall and gazed at the receiver—Marantz, along with an Akai cassette deck. Who played cassettes anymore? A Yamaha turntable and an Akai reel-to-reel-player?

"Nick, my grandfather had one of those. All that's missing here is an eight-track player. My grandfather had one of those, too."

Nick opened the smoked glass cabinet door and showed her the eight-track. Veronica clasped her hands together and laughed.

"That's wonderful! Why Nick, you're a hardcore audiophile."

Nick smiled that devastating, sexy smile she'd not seen since their date at the beach.

"Guilty as charged."

She walked down the length of music and movies. Veronica pulled out a few albums.

"Is it all classic rock?"

Nick stood next to her. "Mostly, but I also like blues and classical. I own some newer rock, but not much. I have a few Miles Davis, though I'm not real big on jazz. I have Sinatra."

Veronica turned and glanced up at him. "I love Frank Sinatra!"

"Good to know."

She put the albums back and moved further down the wall, he had a fifty-inch television on a stand. A dark burgundy leather sofa sat against the window, and a large burgundy leather recliner was angled toward the TV, no doubt his chair.

Veronica inhaled. The room smelled as he did, quality leather mixed with his sexy, unique scent. Next to the television, there was a small bar caddy that looked like it could be from the sixties. A few crystal decanters and matching glasses sat on the top. Below were a few bottles of liquor. She recognized a bottle of Black Bush only because her father used to like it. Somehow, that comforted her. Classic movie posters in frames hung on the walls. *The Big Sleep. Bridge on the River Kwai. Stalag 17.*

"Oh, Nick. I love old movies. You've quite a few here I adore." She smiled.

The movies were in alphabetical order as was the music. Meticulous and organized, his media treated with a lot of loving care.

"This isn't what I imagined."

Nick's face darkened. "Oh? Did you think I lived like a pig? Motorcycle engine parts all over the place, empty pizza boxes on the floor, Doritos crumbs on the rug, and pictures of naked women on the wall? Is that what you thought?"

Veronica turned toward him. What in hell brought that on? She cupped his face and made him look at her.

"Stop it, Nick. I didn't think any such thing at all. Don't be so defensive."

*

Nick glanced down into her determined face. She was right. He was being defensive. He had never brought anyone here before so he supposed he felt nervous and wanted her approval for some reason, a validation of his worth. Why he felt so damned vulnerable around her never ceased to amaze him. He cared what she thought of him and his life.

"Sorry," he mumbled.

She leaned up to lay a soft kiss on his lips.

"Your place is wonderful, Nick. I love it. It says so much about you. Will you show me the rest?"

The kiss and her soft words calmed his insides.

"Sure."

Taking her hand, he showed her the small kitchen and the even smaller bathroom. He only had a shower, no tub. The bedroom was next. Along one wall were bookcases jammed with books on all matter of subjects that interested him, fiction and nonfiction alike. Books on science, history, geography, paranormal, you name it. Along the other wall sat a desk with a computer and a widescreen monitor. He noticed her gaze flitted over to the king-size bed.

"I like lots of room. And if you are wondering, I've never brought a woman back here to my bed. I always went to their place, easier to leave that way."

Ronnie turned to face him. "Nick, I'm sorry I was so—cold—the other night after we had sex. Maybe that old song is right. Live for today, take pleasure while we can."

Nick's heart thumped like mad against his rib cage. He didn't bring her back here for sex, didn't know why, really. Was it to show he wasn't an animal despite outward appearances? Why did he care what she thought? He never cared before what a woman thought of him and his behavior or how he lived. So why now, why her? He never showed any woman this side of him.

He cradled her face. "I'm sorry, too. The sex was intense and I didn't know how to handle it."

"It was intense for me too, Nick. I'm not that experienced. I've only been with a few men in my life. It was nothing like that. Nothing."

"I'll take you home. You'll have to get up in a few hours." He stepped back.

Ronnie continued to hold his gaze. "So where does this leave us, Nick? Are we seeing each other? Casual? Nothing heavy, a little companionship, maybe watch an old movie once in a blue moon?"

Nick didn't know what to say. His insides were raging as a late summer storm. He wanted a little something more or he never would have brought her here to begin with. Calling her had been an impulsive move on his part, might as well see this through. Speak the truth and try and make sense of his jumbled feelings.

"Let's take it as it comes. Casual is fine with me."

"But not exclusive," she whispered.

"No, Ronnie. Not exclusive. Can you live with that?"

Ronnie turned away, he couldn't see her face, but he had the feeling he hurt her and that wasn't his intention. He was striving to be honest. He'd never been exclusive with any woman before, he didn't want to make a promise he couldn't keep.

"Yes," she replied quietly. "I can live with that. It goes both ways."

That he did not expect. Part of him felt relief at her response, but another had regret at its core. Suddenly, the thought of Ronnie being with another man made his gut clench and left a bitter taste in his mouth. He had the feeling there was more going on between them than either wished to admit to each other—or themselves.

Chapter Nine

Friday arrived, and for a July afternoon it wasn't that warm. A cool breeze swirled off the Chesapeake. At least it kept the oppressive gag-inducing haze from the pulp mill that hung over Rockland to a minimal.

Veronica drove her Mustang to Tyler's apartment on Carmarthen Street. She'd left Julie in charge of the shop. She had proved to be more than capable of being left alone for a few hours. They hadn't known each other that well in high school. Julie was often made fun of and teased mercilessly because of her weight. Veronica finally stepped in between a particularly nasty scene between a bully and a sobbing Julie. Shame had covered her for not doing it sooner. They spoke often the rest of the school year, but when Veronica went off to the University of California, she'd lost contact with Julie and a lot of other people from school. Most of the kids Veronica hung out with no longer lived in Rockland, like her, they'd moved on. The pleasure at being home at last warmed her insides. If she hadn't come back, she wouldn't have her bakery and wouldn't have connected with Nick.

Nickelback wailed away on Q-93 FM on her car radio, she smiled. Nick's voice reminded her of Chad Kroeger, the lead singer of the group, with his rough, gravelly, and sexy timber. She bet Nick could sing if he put his mind to it.

Fantasy #3 concerning Nick: On stage, thrusting those muscular hips, and wailing sexy, suggestive lyrics. Veronica squirmed in her seat. Her determination to be in that damned inviting king-size bed of his with his king-size body wrapped around her just amped up her arousal.

Nick was certainly resolute about keeping things casual between them. Isn't that what she wanted? Yes—or no. Damn it, she was confused. Nick baffled her. Live for today? Not a problem. What was all the talk about the picket fence and the sedan? Guess he put it out there that he'll never be shackled or tied down. At least he was honest, to a point.

Veronica pulled into the parking lot of Tyler's apartment building. They needed to have a talk. If she was going to see Nick on a casual basis she wanted her brother to know.

She parked the car, reached in her purse for her keys, and headed for Tyler's. Slipping the key he'd given her in the door, she climbed the stairs to the second floor.

Veronica knocked, unlocked Tyler's door, and entered.

"Tyler?" she said softly.

"Yeah," he answered.

She found him in the living room, sitting on his sofa, staring out the window with what appeared to be a glass of whisky in his hand.

"Are you all right?" she asked.

"Yeah, you know me, I have my moments. Just thinking about things. You came over to talk, what about?" He placed his drink on the table.

Veronica shook her head. Maybe this discussion wasn't a good idea. "I don't think now's the time."

"It'll keep my mind off my troubles. You came all the way over here, go ahead." He sat back and placed his hands behind his head. "I'm a hell of a listener."

Veronica smiled warmly. "I remember. I guess—I'm seeing someone, sort of."

Tyler raised a golden eyebrow. "Already? Who?"

"Nicholas Crocetti."

Tyler stood abruptly. "Nick Crocetti? That biker trash? Since when? How? Why?"

Veronica sighed. Of course, this would be Tyler's reaction. She now dreaded the rest, whatever Tyler knew about Nick that she didn't.

"Sit down, Tyler. Jeez, overreact why don't you? He came in the bakery, we talked, and he asked me out, simple as that. We went out to dinner. I've been to his place. He wanted to show me the bar and where he lives. Are we going to see each other again? Yes, I'm going to his place tomorrow evening. We're going to watch movies."

"Oh, right. Movies!" Tyler snapped.

"Stop overreacting. You're acting like my father, not my brother."

"Dad would have been mortified. Nick Crocetti."

"Don't you dare bring Dad into this," Veronica whispered. "And don't mention it to Mom. I'll tell her when I'm ready. What's so horrible about Nick? Tell me, what do you know? Or is it only the damned rumors?"

"Isn't that enough? You heard the stories and still you went out with him? What rumors did you hear?" Tyler demanded.

Veronica hated when he used that tone of voice, his *cop* voice.

"That he deals drugs. He denied it, he said he doesn't allow drugs in his bar and I believe him. Have you been in his bar? It's classy in a retro sort of way, not some biker's dive."

"And where do you think he got the money to buy that bar, did he tell you that?"

"He said he had money and borrowed a little from his uncle."

"And how did he make that money?"

"Oh, for Christ's sake, Tyler! Just spit it out, quit dancing around the fire." Veronica cried with frustration.

"After he got out of jail—you did know he was in jail?"

She rolled her eyes. "He told me, he was eighteen and stupid."

"Eighteen—and an adult. He has a record. Anyway, he headed north. Wound up in Newark, New Jersey. For four years he was muscle, a leg breaker for the Lucci family. Fenced stolen goods and might've been involved in a warehouse robbery. He also was the driver for the oldest Lucci son, Salvatore. We have a file on Nick Crocetti and so does the Newark Police Department."

Veronica felt like she'd been hit the face with a two-by-four board.

"Was he arrested for any of this?" she asked softly, her voice shaking.

"No, nothing was proven. He was brought in once by the cops in Newark, but they had nothing on him and he wouldn't talk so he was let go. After that, he wound up back down here and bought the bar," Tyler replied.

"Has Nick broken the law since he returned to Rockland?"

"No."

"I get the impression, though Nick won't talk about it, that he didn't have an easy time of it. I saw nothing in his bar or where he lives that indicates he's up to no good. Tyler, his place is wonderful, classy and modern. He collects classic stereo equipment and music. He has a mind boggling collection of music, records, reel-to-reels, eight-tracks, cassettes, CDs, and the movies …"

Tyler laughed cynically. "How do you think he affords all that media bling? You think he's making that much money from his dinky little bar?"

Veronica blinked. It never crossed her mind. Her heart contracted in pain. Was Nick a closet thug? She suddenly felt sick.

Tyler must've seen the devastated look flutter across her face, for he touched her arm gently. "You care about him, don't you? Just how much? Are you in love with him?"

"Love? No! I mean, I barely know him. It's only been two weeks, if that." She gulped. "I care, Tyler. I'm trying not to."

"You had sex with him. Jesus, Ronnie. He's not your type. Does it seem a coincidence that you pick a guy the polar opposite of William Titus with his Brooks Brothers suits?"

"Look, I know I made a mistake with William Titus, I know the pitfalls. I won't mistake great sex for love ever again. I won't allow myself to be hurt here. We're keeping it casual, both of us agree."

Tyler shook his head. He picked up the rest of his drink, threw it back, and his face grimaced at the burn.

He grabbed his shoulder where he'd been shot and winced. "Be careful, Ronnie, for god's sake."

*

That night at Nick's bar, he kept his intense gaze focused on another man with an Irish accent. This guy had been in the bar the last couple of nights. Why these Irish were here in town he couldn't figure out. The blue-collar jobs they used to jump the pond for had all but dried up in the last decade. Granted, Nick read Ireland's economy wasn't doing so well, but he didn't see the need for these guys to come here looking for work. Unless things were worse than he thought.

Was this prick looking to sell drugs like that dead-eyed bastard did last week? Nick watched him closely. The man was nearly as tall as him, but slimmer. Nick could see the muscles under his sweater. This guy would be no pushover. He, like the other Irish, had long hair to his shoulders, hair any woman would envy. It was thick, wavy, and a shade of mahogany brown, almost the color of Nick's wood floors. The man could almost be categorized as pretty, but those blue-green eyes showed no real warmth. Irish had an aura of shrewd menace about him. Enough speculation, Nick threw down his bar towel and strode to the man's table where he sat alone.

"Get you another beer?" Nick asked in a clipped tone.

"Aye, why not? And get one for yourself while you're at it," the man replied in a sing-song, lyrical, Irish accent.

Nick returned with two beers and sat at the table. He told Kevin to stay behind the bar. Friday night was Nick's busiest night. Usually both he and Kevin worked.

"I had another Irish in here a few nights ago, dead-eyed prick with crisscross scars on his face with hair as long as yours, only black. Know him?"

"Depends, what's he done or said?"

"Tried to sell drugs in my place. I told him to take it out to the alley. He didn't like it much."

"I'll not lie, mate. He's my feckin' cousin, Ronan McCarthy. Sorry he caused you grief. He doesn't like to be told what to do."

Nick snorted in disgust. "Yeah, I got that. Basically told me to fuck off. I wanted to snap his spine. Your name McCarthy, too?"

"No, I'm Lorcan Byrne. And you are—?"

"Nick Crocetti, this is my place. I don't allow drugs in here, using or selling. Just so you know."

Nick could see Byrne looking him over and sizing him up.

"Fair play. My cousin and I aren't exactly close. Has he been back?"

Nick shook his head. "No."

Lorcan shrugged. "Well, if he does, snap away, mate. I'll not kick." Lorcan inclined his head toward the pool table. "How about a game?"

Nick considered it, why not? "Rack 'em up, Irish. We could make this interesting."

Lorcan laughed. "Ah, mate. Sounds like you wish to bet some nicker. How about fifty dollars a game?"

"Sounds fair. Best of five. And the loser also buys a round. For the bar."

Lorcan laughed again. "Thank Christ there's only eight guys in here. Just don't be calling all your mates over if I should lose."

Nick stood by and watched Lorcan shoot the breaking ball. Yeah, mates. Like who? Nick had been a loner all his life. He never let anyone get close. So why let this guy? A kindred spirit perhaps. What was the harm of game of pool?

As the night progressed, Lorcan kept up his light-hearted banter, fed the jukebox, and selected songs Nick could find no fault with. He found he liked the guy.

They talked, joked, and played pool. Both were considerably skilled. Each kept winning games. They were tied two apiece when they started the fifth and final game.

Lorcan took his final shot. Applause broke out in the bar for they had attracted quite a crowd. Bets were being passed back and forth, intermixed with the applause were a few moans.

"You won, Lorcan, fair and square. Great game, sit at the bar and I'll get you a drink."

Lorcan's mouth quirked. "Irish whisky, perhaps?"

"No, but I'll tell you what. I'll get some in just for you. Even get that creamy Irish ale, too. You'll come back, a rematch?"

Lorcan nodded. "Aye, I'll be back. You still have to explain baseball to me yet."

"A round on the house!" Nick yelled above the din. Cheers broke out as the men all bellied up to the bar.

And so it began. As unlikely a friendship as either could imagine.

Chapter Ten

Saturday night and Nick had his employee covering the bar for him. Kevin was flexible and dependable. What more could you as for in an employee? Picking Ronnie up on his motorcycle was becoming pure damned torture, not even back to his place yet and his arousal roared at a high temperature. Having her wrapped around his body on the back of his bike affected him. Nick wasn't sure he could last through a movie or two. He wanted her now, in his bed, above him, under him, and in front of him. All night. The swiftness and depth of his desire stunned him.

After a quick peek in the bar, he noticed Kevin seemed to be handling things fine as usual, so he lead Ronnie up the stairs. He hung her light jacket in his closet. He took her hand; his thumb caressed the top as he led her to the movies on the shelves.

"Pick one out," he rasped huskily.

Ronnie scanned the shelves and studied the titles. Damn, she looked beautiful. He loved it when she wore her hair down as she did tonight. She wore black jeans and a silk blouse, a light peach color that complimented her skin.

Finally sensing his gaze, she shyly looked up at him.

"Hi," Nick whispered.

He heard it, a tiny moan bubbled up her throat. That slight sound nearly brought him to his knees. To hell with watching a movie. He cupped her face and began to kiss her, passionately, thoroughly, and more deeply than he had any woman, even with her. Nick flicked his tongue at the corner of her lush, freckled lips and she immediately opened and invited him into her warmth. He then ran his hands down her sides until they cupped her rear. He lifted and brought her right against his iron-hard shaft.

Ronnie threw her arms around his neck and moaned. Their tongues danced seductively, they all but inhaled each other. Nick wrapped her legs around his waist, his hands supporting her ass.

He pulled his lips away enough to gasp, "No movie?"

Ronnie kissed his face, her hands roamed through his hair.

"No movie."

Nick ran toward his bedroom while Ronnie kissed him frantically. He lowered her, and her body ran down the whole long length of him while her toes felt for the floor.

He cupped her face again, a gesture he could not seem to stop. He gazed at her face and studied every adorable freckle. Her glasses slid down her nose, he laughed. He gently removed them and laid them on the end table.

"Can you make love without your glasses?" he whispered. "If not, I'll put them back on because I want you to see everything I'm going to do to you, and with you."

*

Veronica gazed at Nick, never seen such emotion in his eyes. He usually guarded his feelings. He probably wasn't even aware he showed them. Could she see desire, yearning, and maybe more? Or maybe her blurry eyes let her see something that wasn't there.

"We'd better keep them nearby, just in case."

Nick started undoing the buttons on her blouse.

"I've fantasies about you," he growled. "Wearing a certain outfit. Do you want me to show you?"

Well, that sparked her curiosity.

"All right, it won't take long will it?"

Nick jumped into his large, leather swivel office chair in front of his computer. He brought it out of sleep mode and typed the address in the URL line, his long fingers clicking away on the mouse.

"Only take a minute," he murmured.

Veronica picked up her glasses off the desk and put them on, then looked over his shoulder.

"You know the website address by heart?"

"Yep."

He gave one last click and a picture appeared on the screen. She leaned in closer. Her breasts touched his shoulder. Nick moaned.

"Sorry," she laughed, backing up a bit.

"Don't be."

"Nick—is that—a girdle?"

Veronica couldn't believe it. He was on a vintage lingerie site. *Lingerie for that feminine, classic look.*

"It's a sort of girdle, a corselet if you will." He reached around and brought her to stand between his spread legs, his hands roamed all over her body. "You've got the curves, baby, to pull that look off."

Veronica stared at the model. She wasn't skinny, but she wasn't fat either. The outfit was all white, from the body-hugging open girdle to the garters, white stockings and white high heel shoes. The model also wore sheer white gloves past the elbow and a string of glistening white pearls. Very classic indeed, it was right out of the fifties. Well, Nick was certainly full of surprises.

"You like lingerie, then?" she teased.

"On the right woman? Oh yeah," he moaned.

Veronica walked out of his roaming embrace and left the room.

*

What the hell just happened? Was she leaving? Did he gross her out? He knew there were women who didn't like to dress up in anything sexy, was she one of them? A wave of disappointment crushed him and his erection. His cock deflated faster than a punctured balloon. He sat back in his chair in shock, uncertain what to do or say next.

Suddenly, Ronnie returned holding her wallet. She took out a credit card and tossed it to him. He caught it and placed it on his desk.

"Order it, Size 36D. My treat. Have it delivered here and then you can surprise me with it."

His dick sprang back to life in a nanosecond.

"Come here."

He spread his legs far apart so part of the swivel seat showed.

"Sit here, we'll order it together."

"On one condition, lingerie boy," Ronnie crooned.

"Name it, anything."

"I want you to play a little dress-up for me in return, only fair wouldn't you say?" Ronnie picked up her credit card and ran it suggestively over his straining erection. Nick swallowed hard.

"I won't wear lingerie," he croaked.

Ronnie threw back her head and laughed, he loved it when she did that. She had a deep, throaty, husky, sexy laugh. Full-bodied, just like her. Her laugh went straight to his dick hardening it to the point of pain.

"Nick, you're so funny when you put your mind to it. No, not lingerie. I want to see you wearing a kilt and nothing else. Holding a sword. You have a sword, don't you?" She trailed her fingers across his crotch. "We can get you one. You see, Nick, I've a weakness for historical romances, anything with *Highlander* in the title. Hunky, shirtless, laddies wearing kilts on the cover. You should see my collection. So, is it a deal?"

Nick smiled. "Och, I dinna know ye were such a braw lassie. Aye, I agree."

He watched Ronnie's eyes widen at his perfect Scottish burr. Nick was a pretty good mimic if he could say so himself.

"Promise me. You'll talk to me just like that, when we get the kilt," she moaned.

"You want me to be Connor Macleod, William Wallace, or Rob Roy? Baby, I can do it, no sweat. Now, come here." He pulled her over to sit in front of him in the large chair. "And order that—now."

*

Veronica nearly bounced with glee, he agreed! That Scottish accent he used, Oh wow, she was turned on. Her fingers glided over the keys as she typed in her information. Nick's erection was persistent and so were his hands, making it hard to concentrate. He reached around and cupped her breasts. He began to undo the rest of the buttons on her blouse. Pushing it off her shoulders, his warm lips trailed hot, passionate kisses on her arms, his teeth nipping her skin.

"Hurry," he insisted.

Veronica's hands shook as she placed the order. She turned around in the chair and straddled him.

"Done. We'll order the kilt later before I leave, deal?"

"Oh, yeah," he moaned, capturing her mouth with his.

His kiss was insistent. Nick unsnapped her black satin bra and removed it. His lips left hers and moved straight to her breasts.

"God, Ronnie. They're so beautiful."

He captured a nipple in his mouth, he laved, sucked, kissed, and worshipped. Veronica arched her back. His insistent lips felt fantastic. He captured the other breast with his free hand. Nick traveled back and forth between the two, the sensation off the charts. It went on and on until she felt it, she was going to come—just from him sucking her breasts? That never happened before, it nev—

"Oh, Jesus. Niiiccckkkk!"

Veronica screamed her climax. She bet they heard her down in the bar. Nick stood and pulled his sweater off.

Trying to recover her voice, she whispered hoarsely, "Wait, I want to watch you take off your clothes." She climbed onto his bed and laid back completely unconcerned she was bare breasted. "Slowly, Nick. Let me savor you."

Nick sauntered to the computer and brought up a folder.

"Let's make it even better. You might as well know that I like rock sex."

"Rock sex?"

"I like to pound away to the beat of rock music. Another time perhaps, but for now, we'll use this one song for strip music."

The opening rock beat of Foghat's *Slow Ride* filled the room. Nick moved his hips suggestively, slowing undoing his jeans, and pushing them down and kicking them off until he stood in his boxer briefs.

Thrusting in time to the music, he began to grind away in his underwear, hands behind his head like a skilled Chippendale's dancer, flexing his ample biceps much to Veronica's delight. She almost wet herself laughing. Never in her wildest dreams did she imagine sex could be this much fun. To find a man you could laugh with even in the most intimate moments, and never, ever, did she imagine it would be with a man like Nick Crocetti.

Veronica clapped and giggled at his antics. Oh, he was wonderful. He acted goofy and sexy, and it was dammed endearing.

Nick couldn't have timed it more perfectly as the song ended he stood before her completely nude. She stopped laughing. The man was masculine, muscular perfection. What a surprise, he didn't have any tattoos or piercings that she could see. She dare not verbalize it aloud, for she surmised Nick might take offence.

Oh yeah, I have a motorcycle, I was in jail, I should be covered in tattoos, she could hear him sneer. It would be a mood killer to be sure. Besides, Nick wasn't turning out the way she imagined on so many levels. No, she'd keep that particular observation to herself. The room became deathly quiet. He stood and leaned on one hip, his eyes hooded with passion, his body hard and ready.

Nick strolled to the light switch. He turned the dial on the dimmer, washing the room in a soft, dusky twilight.

Veronica suddenly felt self-conscious and reached for a pillow and held it in front of her, hiding her bare torso.

Walking back toward the foot of the bed, he crawled up the bed toward her like a tiger stalking his prey. His muscles flexed and bunched as he moved. The fun and laughter seemed to be over. Nick looked serious. His face showed his hunger, his need, and it all but took her breath away. He reached for the pillow she clutched tightly. Veronica struggled to hold it, but only for a minute. He tossed it aside.

"Never hide yourself. Not with me," he whispered. He tugged on her jeans. "Take these off."

She unzipped them, arched her hips upward, and pushed them down. Nick grabbed both legs and pulled them the rest of the way off. She was left only in her black satin panties. His hands roved over her legs and spread them wide. He stroked and caressed her skin, his breathing puffing out as a steam engine. He lay down on his stomach, his face inches from her crotch.

Veronica started to tremble from anticipation. He reached in under the thin satin with his long, talented fingers and teased her curls.

"You're so wet," he moaned.

Nick moved all around her folds. He pulled his fingers out and languidly licked them. "And taste so sweet."

Veronica had never seen a man do that. He tasted her like sweet maple syrup. She thought it would sicken her, but it didn't, it made her more aroused.

"Are these panties expensive? A favorite pair?" He asked with a sexy wicked grin.

"No, not really—"

Nick gripped her panties and ripped them right off her body.

"Oh, my *god*!" she cried out.

Nick spread her legs further, and before she could even take a deep breath, he laved at her folds, drinking and sucking. His tongue moved in and out with decided purpose. William Titus had done this once to her that wild, wedding weekend, but not with this finesse, this—talent. Nick's technique was pure magic. With two fingers he spread her folds wide.

"Beautiful," he murmured. "I want you to come for me, Ronnie. Scream all you want, no one will hear. I told Kevin to keep the jukebox downstairs cranked wide open. Scream for me."

Nick devoured her like a rich, decadent dessert. He savored and delighted in her essence.

Her back arched, the sensual sensation built into something William Titus could not bring her to. The pending climax like nothing she'd experienced before. Not better than another orgasm she had, but on a different scale, a different damned universe. Veronica splintered apart. Everything went dark. She opened her mouth to scream, but only a dry croak came out. Her head bounced up and down on the pillow as she shuddered, over and over. A *multiple* orgasm—her first.

Nick. She knew it would be with Nick.

Chapter Eleven

Nick watched her reaction with satisfaction. He never saw anything so sexy as Ronnie climaxing. This one was intense he could tell; she still shuddered. He touched her and she shook and trembled again. Smiling, he leaned down and took the hard nub into his mouth. Ronnie came again, within minutes. He could drive her wild like this for hours, but he wanted inside this wet, exotic place of hers. If he could crawl up inside her—he would.

Nick stood on his knees, his face and goatee glistening with her essence. He reached to the end table and slid open the drawer, bringing out the box of condoms. He wiped his mouth and smiled at her.

"Sweet, juicy nectar. Sweetest I've ever tasted."

He pulled out a package, ripped it open, and rolled the condom over his cock. Still on his knees, he moved closer and gripped her hips. Nick tilted her slightly upward and plunged into her. He groaned loudly. So damned wet, but wonderfully tight, her inner muscles clenched him. Nick took one of her legs and rested it on his hip as he thrust deeper. He soon settled into a slow, languid rhythm she easily matched. God, this was more intense than the wild animal sex behind her bakery if that were even damned possible.

He closed his eyes. Nothing—nothing compared to this sweet, wet torture. He let out a moan that sounded like a wolf baying at the moon and he didn't care.

Damn, he could do this for hours. He slowed briefly, savoring the feel of her clutching, milking, and caressing his cock. He leaned forward until he could feel that hard nub, swollen and rubbing against him. It demanded further release, it screamed for it. He let out a feral growl. More, he wanted more.

Nick threw her shapely legs over his shoulder. He had to go deeper. As deep as he could go, buried, masked, and obscured by her hot, wet core.

She gasped. "Nick …What—"

His hand stroked one of her legs.

"You'll love this, baby, hold on. I'm going to go so deep inside of you, I will touch your soul."

He nibbled hungrily on her leg and couldn't believe he just said that. But Christ, she felt so good, so right. He wanted to give Ronnie pleasure— deep, throbbing bliss. He found he *did* want to touch her soul.

He moved faster, rotating his hips at her tilted ones. He was so deep. His breath was ragged and out of control. How many times had he had sex over the years? This was near a religious epiphany, or so he imaged. Intense. Wrenching. Powerful. All consuming.

Fucking fantastic.

*

Veronica watched as Nick pounded away. His head was thrown back, every cord in his neck pulled tight and strained as if he reached for something. His perfectly shaped white teeth were clenched. He gasped and moaned, verbalizing in a raw, unfiltered way what he was doing and what he would do next. Dirty talk from Nick. She loved that gravelly deep voice.

"I'm going to fuck you all night, Ronnie. My hard, aching cock deep, buried so deep—"

As for her, she'd just experienced another release. What was that, four or five times? How could he keep this up? This must be the stamina part she'd heard about. The man was insatiable.

He went achingly slow, then so fast. Veronica was inundated with pure, raw pleasure-torture. Her body throbbed with want and need. Her hair was a sweaty mass of tangles, plastered to her forehead. How much time passed, she had no idea.

A look of pure gratification crossed his handsome features. Veronica had to admit she was secretly pleased to see his desire showing on his face. She moved her hips a little quicker. Nick opened his eyes and gazed down at her.

"Faster … harder?" he murmured.

Veronica couldn't speak; she could only nod. Without withdrawing from her, he lowered her legs and gently turned her over so she lay on her stomach. He lifted her to her hands and knees. The skill at which he managed that deft move was impressive. Nick—if nothing else—was very good at this. She tried not to think of the fact he'd been with so many damned women before her. Veronica felt his hands clasp hers. Nick placed them on his headboard.

He leaned in and whispered in her ear, "Hold on, baby. Fast and hard. Or should I say, faster and harder?"

The slow withdraw, right to the tip, and then he plunged in to the hilt. A ragged cry tore from her throat from the intensity and pure contentment. This was fast becoming her favorite position, Nick behind her. It was so carnal and untamed. Like him.

He pumped harder, his hips rotating as he did. Skin slapped against skin, her breasts heaved back and forth from the sensation of him banging away. Nick grasped her rear tightly. She could feel it. Ripples of dark and light colors burst behind her eyes and a ragged cry tore from her throat. Seconds later, Nick followed her onto that unknown celestial sphere. He gripped her taut against him while he shuddered and roared. He bucked and quaked for interminable moments.

He slowly withdrew. Still on his knees, he turned her to face him and cupped her cheeks. His strong hands on her face kept her upright.

"Ronnie," he exhaled. "Stay with me tonight. Let me love you, all night. Sleep in my arms."

Nick, *casual sex, love 'em and leave 'em* Crocetti just asked her to spend the night? She was stunned. He sounded almost—vulnerable. Surely, she imagined it, but the invitation was too good to pass up as he may never make it again.

"All right, Nick."

He leaned in to touch her forehead with his. He laughed.

"I'm ready to go again, how about you?"

Veronica glanced down, still semi-hard. Stamina. Wow. She reached down to remove the used rubber. Nick quivered slightly at the contact.

"Wastebasket, over there."

She dropped it in a lined basket, and then reached by the bedside for another condom. Together, they slipped it over his cock.

"Guess I'm ready to go again, too." She pushed him down on the bed. "Let me touch you Nick, please."

Nick lay back on the pillow, hands behind his head. He smiled wickedly.

"Explore away. Touch wherever you want, whatever you want."

She sat upright on his lower thighs, she roved her hands over his broad shoulders, his impressive tightly packed pectorals, and his bulging biceps. As she brushed past his nipples, they hardened, her fingers lingered on the golden-brown hair on his upper chest. Oh, so soft. A little hair on a man's chest appealed. Nick had just enough—of everything.

She moved lower toward his muscled abdomen, six pack—big time. The man was amazingly fit, perfectly muscled, and a glorious specimen of a man. What every man should aspire to. Veronica wondered how he managed to stay so fit. He didn't play sports that she knew of. Maybe he just hit the genetic jackpot.

The part of his body that amazed her the most was his cock. It was just the right size for her. Nick stretched her in ways she didn't think possible. The feeling of fullness was indescribable. Veronica grabbed his shaft. There was so much of him, and long enough that he could go deep and touch her in that sweet spot without hurting her. Perfect. His cock twitched in her hand and a long, languid moan escaped from Nick's lips. That from-the-toes moan of his she loved to hear. The sound sent tremors down her spine.

"Ride me, baby."

She slowly lowered herself on his rock-hard erection. Nick moved his hands from behind his head and placed them on either side of her hips. The feel of those warm, large, masculine hands had branded her.

Veronica rocked back and forth. The feel of him, inside, so deep. Nick moved his hips up and down in harmony with her motions. Nick sat up slightly to capture one of her breasts with his mouth. The sensations that inundated her were hard to absorb.

She placed a couple more pillows behind Nick to keep him in an upright position, and to keep him at her breasts. He moved from one to the other. She came, a star-bursting orgasm. Nick wouldn't give an inch; he kept sucking and laving.

Out of the corner of his mouth he rasped, "Keep going—again."

She was boneless like a damned jellyfish, but she kept rocking. He spoke the truth. Surely she'd burst a vein in her head.

Was Nick saying something? Her brain tried to clear the sex haze. He wanted her to go faster. She had no idea where she found the strength. Her release slammed her hard and she cried out.

"Jesus!" Nick growled.

His body tensed as he came. Next thing she knew, Nick laid her next to him and moved her limp arm across his chest. He curled her in next to him and laid her head on his shoulder.

"Sleep, baby," he whispered.

Sleep? She felt hung over. Limp like a rag doll, but utterly and completely satisfied and damned happy. Her fingers curled through the damp hair on his chest, her lids lowered and she fell asleep.

*

Nick opened one eye. He glanced at his digital clock. The time read 3:18 A.M. Ronnie was still asleep and wrapped around him as snug as a comforting quilt. Damn, he hated to disturb her, but he had to piss. He slowly extricated himself and she moaned and turned over, but didn't wake. Nick padded to the bathroom, lifted the cover of the bowl, and relieved himself.

Splashing a little water on his face, he looked in the mirror. The best-damned sex he ever had.

The bar closed at two in the morning, Kevin no doubt locked up and went home. His place didn't open again until twelve noon. He supposed he should take Ronnie home before then. Maybe he should wake her now and take her home. Nick never should've asked her to stay, what possessed him?

Nick walked back to the bed, lay down, leaned up on one elbow, and watched her. Ronnie looked serene, peaceful, and sated. This woman was gorgeous, inside and out. Her lush, pliable, eager body was everything he wanted physically in a woman. Her face was beautiful and luminescent. Those blue-gray eyes of hers watched him so studiously, no doubt trying to figure him out. The fact she was also funny, smart—and could bake—ramped up her attractiveness to him. He smiled. He pulled her against him so she curved into his body. His body stirred to life at the contact. She wriggled and sighed. Her luxuriant ass hardened him further. Nick leaned down and kissed her cheek.

"Nick?"

"Who else would it be," he teased.

Nick moved his hips so she could feel his arousal. He felt a condom package being thrust into his hand. He laughed and tore open the package. Slipping it on, he nudged her from behind. Ronnie spread her legs and he slid right in, straight into her feminine core. Staying in the spoon position, he moved in and out of her with slow, sensual glides. Some minutes passed and they both came to a gentle, soul-stirring climax.

He stayed inside her and fell asleep. A deep restful slumber, the best he had in years.

Chapter Twelve

Veronica opened one eye. The clock's large red numbers read eight minutes past nine. Next to her, the space was empty. A noise out in the kitchen area pinpointed Nick's location.

She stretched languorously like a lazy cat that had been sleeping in the sun, even spread her toes in contentment. Veronica hadn't slept this late in ages. Of course, she didn't get much sleep the night before.

Nick must have laid a throw over her sometime this morning. Last she remembered, they were both naked and joined. She tried to move her legs, and muscles she didn't even know she possessed groaned in protest. It felt as if—he was still inside her. Veronica inhaled deeply, the room smelled of musky sex or maybe it was her. She needed a shower. Thank god there was a connecting door from his bedroom.

She glanced out the window through the half-open blinds. The day couldn't be more beautiful. Veronica felt like opening the window and singing to the blue sky above while birds landed on her outstretched hands and joined her in a song of joy. She giggled at the absurdity of the scene, straight out of an animated fairy-tale. She felt like a princess this morning, how long that feeling would last is another question.

Cupboard doors slammed in the kitchen. Yes, she had the feeling Nick Crocetti would act the same way he did the last time they had sex, cool and detached. Well, this morning she wasn't going to sit by and let him shut himself down emotionally.

Swinging her legs out of bed, she groaned slightly from the play on her muscles, gathered her clothes, and ran into the bathroom. After relieving herself, she had a look around. The bathroom was a very small room that had been recently renovated. She opened the medicine cabinet. There were five boxes of condoms on the top shelf. *Five? What did he do, buy them by the gross?* A sharp pain clutched her heart.

Again, the thought that she stood in a very, very long line galled her to no end. How many other women had been here? Did he lie when he said she was the first in his bed? She locked the bathroom door, then got down on her haunches and began digging through the vanity for anything remotely feminine, tweezers, Lady Bic razor, sanitary pads, or used lipstick. She dug through the neatly folded towels, nothing. Veronica stood and inspected the medicine chest again, condoms, Band-Aids, Aspirin, aftershave, dental floss, deodorant, and antiseptic. Guilt flushed her cheeks. What kind of woman goes through a man's personal things? A paranoid one, apparently.

She closed the door and glanced in the mirror. A single tear zig-zagged down her cheek. It'd be so easy to fall for Nick Crocetti. She wiped the lone tear away and leaned in to turn on the water in the shower. Veronica had to keep control of her emotions. She was so damned afraid of being hurt again and so determined to make sure this casual sex didn't turn into something more. *Good luck with that,* she muttered as she stepped under the cascading water.

*

Nick stood in the middle of his small kitchen undecided as what to do next. He heard the water running in the shower. It took all his willpower not to slip into the bathroom and join her even though he had his already. He groaned aloud at the thought of soaping up those succulent curves of hers and his body stirred to life, again. Closing his eyes, he splayed his hands on the marble countertop. *Get control.*

Nick felt awkward. Never should have asked her to stay. He wasn't used to someone else occupying his private space. The feeling was damned unsettling. No doubt caught up in the moment. He'd never slept with anyone before. Strange, considering the number of sex partners he had through the years. He always went to the woman's place and left right after, no cuddling, no affection, no staying the night and sleeping in each other's arms. Staying overnight was too intimate, too personal. It would start him on that road he'd no intention of traveling, toward companionship, relationship, and love. So why her? As determined as he was to keep her at arm's length, she kept slipping past his defenses, his well-structured, reinforced barrier that wrapped around his heart.

Sunday mornings he usually cooked himself a full brunch, eggs with cheese, ham or bacon, hash browns, toast, the whole enchilada. Should he do it for her? Again, it seemed too—personal. Nick lifted his head and glanced at the box she brought from the bakery, half-dozen cinnamon buns. Give her a bun, coffee, then whisk Ronnie the hell out of here.

He padded to the coffee maker and measured out a breakfast blend he liked. He reached for two plates and placed them on his small table in the corner. When he woke around eight o'clock, Ronnie was sound asleep and curled up in his arms. It felt so damned good—so right. A feeling he could get used to. It would've been so easy to wake her up and make love to her again. Nick awoke in an aroused state because of what they'd shared. *Laughter, goofiness and passion.*

What stunned him was Ronnie ordered the lingerie to please him. Damn, that rocked him to his soul. His strip tease, what in hell brought that on? She loved it, she laughed and clapped. The look of pure delight on her face pleased him to no end. Nick didn't plan it, it just—happened. He usually wasn't so spontaneous or comical. Ronnie said he could be funny. He had no damned idea he could be. New emotions rolled through him, unknown sensations. He couldn't be any more confused.

*

Showered and dressed with her hair still damp, Veronica stepped into the kitchen and her breath caught in her throat. Nick wore nothing but flannel sleep pants. They rode low on his slim, muscular hips. He poured big mugs of coffee, and then turned to face her. She had to fight the urge to run into his arms and hug him tight. Nick motioned to the small table where cinnamon buns sat on a platter along with butter and fresh fruit.

"Good morning, Nick."

"Yeah, good morning," he murmured.

Oh, shit. There was the tightly controlled voice and the shuttered, emotionless face. Veronica wouldn't be intimidated or angered this time by his cool, dismissive tone. Smiling, she walked to the chair and sat.

"It looks lovely, Nick. Nothing like cinnamon buns on a Sunday morning!" she declared brightly.

He strode to the table in his bare feet and placed a large mug of coffee in front of her. All the dishes matched, unlike her mismatched bits and pieces that were stored in her cupboard. Nick sat opposite and buttered his cinnamon bun.

Taking a large sip of coffee she asked, "Nick, you've never mentioned your parents. Do they live around here?"

By the look on his face she might've asked him to pass the cream.

Finally, he responded. "No." Interminable moments passed, and then Nick continued, "My father's in New York City. Last I heard, driving a courier truck. My mother's out west in a small town in Nebraska living with some rancher."

Veronica took a small bite of the bun. "Are they divorced?"

"You really don't want to hear this, and I really don't want to talk about it."

"Maybe I do want to hear it, Nick. Maybe it would do you good to talk about it with someone, why not me? How did you come to be living with your uncle?" She wasn't going to be put off by his icy glare.

Nick took a gulp of coffee, wincing at the burn. "Mom and Dad married because Mom got pregnant. They probably divorced because of me; they made our lives a misery. I suppose I was to blame for that, too. When they finally split, I was seventeen. I was a handful getting into trouble my whole life and neither of them wanted me. Mom called her brother here in Rockland, a total stranger to me and he agreed to take me in. We lived in Newark at the time, though we moved around a lot through the Mid-Atlantic States. Dad never could hold a job," Nick sighed gruffly. "I don't like talking about this, about myself. My childhood sucked: the fights, the upheaval, the poverty, and most of all—the hatred. I've tried to forget it."

"You've no contact with them at all?" Veronica asked softly.

"I get a Christmas card from Mom every Christmas, Dad? No. We're better off, all of us. We've moved on. We weren't meant to be a family. It was all wrong from the beginning." Nick shrugged.

Veronica had the feeling his hurt went deep. To be rejected by your own parents—she couldn't imagine growing up in such a house. Her childhood home had always been filled with love. Her parents loved each other very much; they were always kissing and hugging, even in front of her and Tyler. They all did things together, went on car trips, to Orioles baseball games, and movies. They played board games and watched TV. Sunday night, Mom made popcorn and they watched movies. Each week they took turns selecting the programming. They were all—friends. Veronica wouldn't show too much sympathy here. Nick wouldn't like it. She guessed that much about him. She also wouldn't rub his nose in it that her childhood was close to idyllic. Not perfect, but pretty good as childhoods go.

"And your uncle? What was he like?"

She took another sip of coffee.

"Uncle Henry was a little strange. He never married. He didn't know what to do with me, or say to me. Never had to deal with kids before, not that I was a kid, I turned eighteen after being with him a couple of months. Legally, I was an adult. I could've left, but I had no place to go."

Veronica digested the information. Unwanted and unloved by his own family. Such an upbringing would affect a person right into their adulthood. Could explain why he sometimes seemed detached from emotions even while they had sex, though he obviously enjoyed it. Did a protection mechanism kick in if he felt too much? Who was she to judge? She tried to keep emotion out of this equation as well. Maybe that was a mistake. Or maybe she deluded herself, for she felt plenty here. Why deny it? Simple, she was scared to death of being hurt. Nick made it plain he wasn't the settling down type.

"And when you were sent to jail, where was your uncle?"

Nick popped a green grape in his mouth.

"He left me there to rot and to teach me a lesson. He could've bailed me out; instead he left me there for six months."

Veronica gasped, how could his uncle do that?

"I'm so sorry, Nick."

"Tough love, he called it. There was no love involved. He contacted my parents. My father picked that moment to wash his hands of me. Mom? She sent a couple of letters. She had her own life to lead. She stated the rancher wouldn't want her jailbird son anywhere near, so there was no invite to Nebraska, not that I would've gone."

Veronica laid her hand on top of his. He looked up at her, his eyes glazed with anger and hurt, it was painful for him to talk about this. Maybe she shouldn't have brought it up, but it explained so much. It also raised new questions. Questions that were best left for another day, perhaps.

"You can ask me anything you like, Nick. Only fair."

Nick threaded his long fingers through hers, the contact seared.

"Tell me about your marriage."

Yow, he went right for the jugular.

"Big mistake. I used to work at a consulting firm in San Francisco. William Titus was a real estate mogul and I had been assigned to his account. He was handsome, rich, smart, and I fell for him. Before William, I had very little sexual experience. William opened up a whole new world to me. We wound up going to Las Vegas for a wild weekend. At the end of the trip, we found ourselves at one of those cheesy chapels on the strip and wound up married. I imagined myself in love, thought William felt the same, and then he sobered up. He was mortified to find we were married. His blue blood parents wouldn't stand for it. He told me in no uncertain terms he didn't love me. He wanted my body, nothing more. He accused me of coercing him to the Elvis altar. The whole experience was horrible." Veronica drew in a tight breath. "His family started divorce proceedings. They threw in a large settlement to sweeten the pot. I took it. I used some of the money to buy the bakery. The rest is in the bank. I swore from that day forward, no man would ever hurt me again."

*

Nick's thumb stilled, he stroked the top of her hand as she spoke. It explained a lot. Both of them were a pair. Hurt, damaged. Yeah, he knew he was. He didn't like to admit it to anyone, not even himself.

"You think I'll hurt you, don't you?"

"I don't know," she whispered in a voice so soft he barely heard the words.

"Live for today, Ronnie. That's all I can do."

"So what are we, Nick? Are we seeing each other? A couple? Because I'll be honest with you, what we shared last night is rare. I don't want to walk away; I want to explore it. See where it leads. Am I afraid? Damned straight, but I'm also not a coward. I'm willing to go forward at your pace, take one day at a time, live for today as you say."

Nick sat back in his chair and pulled his hand away.

"I don't know if I want that—ever. A relationship."

"In other words, you can't pledge any kind of fidelity here, is that what you're saying? I know about all the women, Nick. If I'm just another notch on the bedpost tell me now, so I can avoid that hurt."

Nick's heart clenched in his chest. "No, you're not another notch. I never would've asked you to stay all night."

Ronnie bit her lower lip. "At the bakery in the alley, after we—you were distant, cold even. You got what you wanted, you could've moved on, why didn't you?"

Nick shook his head. "You want an honest answer? I don't know. It was my original plan to walk away. I'm a cold-hearted bastard, Ronnie. No use denying it. Emotions and feelings don't factor much into my actions, especially where sex and women are concerned. I like sex, I always have. It's not natural for men to be faithful. It's not the nature of the beast."

Ronnie laughed a short, dismissive sort of laugh. "Oh, please. That's what men say to justify their behavior. Is there another woman already?"

He noticed the slight tremble in her voice, as though she fought to keep control.

"No, Ronnie. There's been no other woman since we hooked up. But I can't say there never will be. I would be lying if I did, and I don't want to lie to you, ever."

"Yes, you've been honest. Then let me be honest as well. There is something between us, perhaps it's only great sex and maybe it's more. I'd like to find out. If you can't pledge fidelity than neither will I."

Nick exhaled. *Jesus.* His brain was swimming. Swirling, confused emotions enveloped him. She deserved honesty. Hell, the time had come for him to be honest with himself. He didn't want her seeing other men. The mere thought of it made him want to pound the unknown guy into hamburger meat. His heart thudded in his chest just thinking about the possibility. He ran his hands through his hair in frustration. So he would lay off the women. Or try to.

"Okay, I'll move forward, Ronnie. We will be an exclusive couple—for now. But I can't be rushed or smothered. Can you let me move at my own pace here?"

Ronnie stood, and kissed him gently on the forehead.

"That's fine. I'm in no rush either. You decide when you want us to see each other again. You better take me home."

Suddenly, the thought of her leaving squeezed his heart, which felt strange because only an hour ago he wanted her the hell out of here.

"Don't you want to finish your coffee? Talk a little more? I don't have to open until noon. Stay, Ronnie."

She cocked her head at him, her hand on her hip. "Are you sure? I don't want to smother you."

He laughed and pointed to the chair. "Sit down, relax. You know, that took guts what you did. Quit your cushy corporate job, move back home, and start a business in this economy."

Ronnie sat. "Yes, I suppose it did. I always loved baking bread and rolls. I never feel more at peace than when I am up to my elbows in flour and dough. I'm creating something. God, it's such a rush. I've had more satisfaction in my work the last two weeks than I did the whole eight years at Byant Consulting."

Nick reached for another cinnamon bun.

"I know what you mean about being at peace. That's how I feel when I ride my bike. Was it a well-paying job?"

Ronnie tucked her leg up and took another sip of coffee. "I walked away from big money. But I suppose I wanted to distance myself from William Titus and the hurt and humiliation. Besides, I never intended to stay in California. I went out to university there with every intention of coming back after I graduated, but the job opportunity came up. The position was too good to pass up," she sighed. "The years got away from me, then Dad passed—and Mom moved to Florida to live with her older sister. I just put it off, didn't want to face the fact Dad was gone. I still can't believe it."

A tear trailed down her flushed cheek. Nick took her hand.

"I was at the funeral."

Her head snapped up. "You were?"

"I figured you didn't know who I was so I paid my respects from a distance. I saw how devastated you and your whole family were. I'm sorry." He leaned forward and brought her trembling hand to his lips and kissed it tenderly. "You loved him very much, didn't you?"

"Yes," Ronnie sobbed. Tears were flowing freely now. "I'm truly sorry you never knew that kind of love. My father was everything to me. He was my hero. I miss him so much."

Nick's heart clenched once again. Damn, the feelings and emotions roaring through him were staggering. He stood and walked to Ronnie. Lifting her up, he then sat her in his lap. His thumbs brushed away the wayward tears.

"No, I've never known that kind of love. But I'm glad you have. You've wonderful memories, cherish them. It's rare."

Ronnie slipped her arm around his neck and buried her face in his naked chest. She sniffled, the crying slowed to muffled hiccups.

"Have you ever been in love, Nick? Or loved anyone at all?"

He didn't answer for many minutes. She'd ripped open his heart. He could shut down as he always did when talking or thinking about emotions. But with her, he found he didn't want to, at least not in this moment.

"Once—long ago," he whispered. He took a tendril of her hair and absently played with it and then pushed it gently behind her ear. "A woman took pity on a boy who was starving for love and affection. She was four years older than me. I thought her attention meant she loved me. When she threw me aside, I was devastated. I thought my life was over. The feelings were intense as only a first love can be. That's when I drove off and got in trouble."

"The bar fight? Jail?"

"Yeah. It all stemmed from that. Just another rejection. You think I would've been used to it. But, it was the sex. Like what you described with William Titus. So intense, I thought I was in love. I haven't made that mistake since."

Ronnie cupped his cheeks and gazed at him.

"Don't you ever think you're not worthy of love, Nick Crocetti. You are. You've so much to give if only you would let yourself—feel."

She gave him such a gentle and tender kiss. A soothing kiss that a mother would give a small boy who had scraped his knee. Her kiss deepened.

"We could—you know." She inclined her head toward his bedroom.

He couldn't, not now. Not with the way the feelings overwhelmed him. He knew if he took her to his bed he would wind up weeping in her arms. He kissed her nose.

"I'm tempted, but I'd better get dressed and take you home."

He tried to stand, but Ronnie still had a firm hold of his face.

"You'll call, Nick, won't you? When you're ready?"

He smiled, or tried to. His lips felt paralyzed from her caring kiss. "Yes, I will."

*

An hour later, Veronica stood at the front entrance of her bakery as Nick roared off down Waterloo Street.

He kissed her goodbye, a deep, soul-stirring kiss of deep desire. Right, he was keeping emotion out of it. Veronica had the feeling they were both fooling themselves. What they shared last night was beyond her experience. It wasn't just sex, as much as they might pretend otherwise. He wouldn't be rushed or smothered; she could live with that. She wasn't exactly sure what she felt herself.

As she stuck the key in the door she realized they didn't order the kilt before she left. A small sigh of disappointment blew out from her pursed lips. *So much for that.*

Chapter Thirteen

A few days passed and Nick didn't call her, he needed the time to think. When he woke up each morning, disappointment washed through him because Ronnie wasn't curled up next to him. He never thought he would be a cuddler, but Ronnie proved him wrong. He missed her curves and her warmth. She brought him peace. He never slept as deep and as serene as he did the night she lay in his arms.

Nick didn't know what in hell to think about any of it. He walked behind the bar to grab a couple of beers. Lorcan had returned as he had a few times this week. He found he liked the Irishman for all his blarney, he seemed intelligent, and they shared a lot of interests. Lorcan was a year younger, but somehow seemed older. Nick had the feeling Lorcan had done and seen plenty.

Nick walked to the table and placed two cans of Kilkenny on it. He sat opposite Lorcan who cocked an eyebrow at him.

"Kilkenny? Why, Nick mate, thanks. You're going to have one as well? Will wonders ever cease?"

"I've had it before. It's pretty good actually. Full-bodied, lush, but not overpowering."

Lorcan laughed. "Aye, much like the Irish countryside, lush but not overpowering."

Nick raised his can. "Or perhaps like Irish women?"

Lorcan laughed again. "Bang-on mate. Cheers."

They both took a long swig. They'd just finished another game of pool. A Jefferson Airplane song played quietly in the background. There were only a few other guys in the bar as Wednesday was Nick's slowest night.

"So, what brought you to Rockland?" Nick asked.

Lorcan glanced up, his blue-green eyes hardened. "I'll be honest with you, Nick. I'm working for the De Luca's. You know them?"

"Yeah, I've heard of them. Who hasn't?"

Christ. He didn't expect that response. The De Luca's? Lorcan was mixed up in that? He never would've guessed. The alarm in his gut began to ring.

Lorcan took another drink. "My cousin Ronan and I came over with Sullivan McDermott; he's a cousin to the De Luca's on the mother's side. We run the strip club outside of town, The Playpen. You've heard of it?"

Nick sucked air through his teeth. "Yeah, I've been there a few times. I wasn't aware the De Luca's owned it."

"Apparently it's a recent acquirement. They want to expand their legit businesses."

"And that's all you are in, the legit side?" Nick murmured.

"I can't say, Nick. I'd rather not. I like you mate, for the sake of our new friendship it's best not picked at, you follow?"

Nick shrugged. "Listen, I'm no innocent here. I worked for the Lucci family in Jersey for four years. So yeah, I follow. Just let me say my place is clean. I want to keep it that way, understand?"

"Fair play, mate. We understand each other." Lorcan's dimples danced teasingly. "Now, tell me about your wee girl. How'd the date go?"

Nick didn't know what to say. He still wasn't sure himself. He wanted to see her again—a light went on in his brain like someone flicked a switch.

"Listen, Lorcan. I'd like to see her again, but not alone, not now. I need to get a few things sorted. How about we arrange a double date? She has a friend that works with her in the bakery."

"Bloody hell, mate. A fix-up? Do I look desperate?"

"Maybe you'd like to be with a woman who wasn't a stripper for once," Nick taunted good-naturedly.

"What does she look like?"

"Shit, I don't know. I've never seen her. The woman can't be that bad. Come on, this Saturday night. We'll go out for drinks. A couple of hours." Nick urged.

"You must have it bad, mate. Being alone with her sends you all aflutter? I want to meet this woman. All right, a couple of hours. But that's it. No going off and leaving me alone with this bakery assistant, you follow?"

Nick laughed. "Sure, I follow. Her friend's name is Julie. Do I have it bad? I've no damned idea. That's why I need time to think, but I want to see her. Jesus, talk about confused."

And he didn't have any idea. He looked at the Irishman sitting across from him, grinning from ear to ear. Funny, as soon as Ronnie entered his life all of the sudden he had a friend. Something he never really had before. Did Ronnie unlock a part of his heart? Kick a hole in that protective fence? Obviously she did or Nick would've never let Lorcan get close.

*

Shortly after two in the morning, Ronan McCarthy stood out in the parking lot of The Chief. He stayed well out of sight. The bar had closed, he could see the big biker stacking chairs and collecting bottles.

Ronan parked his car around the corner. A cold, stinging rain fell, the type that chills to the bone, but Ronan felt none of it. He had ice water in his veins anyway. He'd not forgotten Nick Crocetti; he was in his book. His book of revenge he had since he was a kid. Anyone mess with him or insult him, *in the book.* When he found his revenge he stroked the name out.

What surprised him was the fact his bloody cousin started hanging out at this bar. He watched as Lorcan left at closing, laughing and talking with the biker at the door. What the feck was going on there? His cousin better not get between him and his plans.

What to do? Setting the place on fire seemed an option. Take away his feckin' source of income and his home all in one fell swoop. Kill the shite? No, that was too harsh for the insult given, though murder had been tempting the night of their confrontation. It was not like he hadn't done it before.

Ronan had his own twisted sense of personal justice and Crocetti's insult did not warrant killing despite his initial reaction. He watched Crocetti stack chairs. The place was closed now. *Big bloody bastard.* Hand-to-hand combat was out, that bruiser would win.

Burning the place looked more of an option. The plan required a good deal of thought. He wasn't an arsonist by trade so he would have to do a little research.

Revenge he would get, no worries there. Then he would strike out his name. No one talked to him the way Crocetti did. No one.

*

After ten in the morning as was now the ritual, Veronica brought out two steaming mugs of tea for her and Julie. This morning they were having Twinings Irish Breakfast Tea. Seemed appropriate for what she had to relay to her friend. Getting comfortable on the stool, Veronica pushed the plate of plain tea biscuits to the middle of the counter.

Julie shook her head. "No, I'd better not."

"There are hardly any calories in them. Take two of them to dunk in your tea. I promise I'll not tempt you with anything else."

Julie laughed. "Okay. You twisted my arm. It's better than those sinful peanut butter cookies and yes, I confess, I had one the other day. They are to die for."

"That's my mother's recipe. Never fails. Julie, Nick called."

"Finally, took him four or five days. He's not going to make this easy, is he?"

Veronica took a bite of the tea biscuit. "No, he isn't. He's asked if you and I would go out with him and a friend."

"The Terminator has a friend? Sorry." She grinned sheepishly.

"I'm surprised as you are. Nick never said a word, must be recent. Anyway, drinks this Saturday night. What do you say?"

Julie looked down into her mug of tea as if it would give her magical insight or answers.

"I don't think so. I haven't been on a date in three years. I'm rusty as hell. A guy I've never seen before?"

"I asked Nick about him. He's Irish and his name is Lorcan Byrne, he's right off the plane from Dublin, accent and everything. Said he's almost as tall as him, at least an inch or so over six feet."

"Well, at least he's not a leprechaun," Julie murmured. "I hate to ask this, but what about his looks?"

"Well, I didn't want to ask and Nick never really said. You know men. He would've been useless describing him. He's thirty, Irish, or did I mention that? Even I'm intrigued. The accent alone would have me interested," Veronica teased.

*

Julie didn't like it. She never liked blind dates, or fix-ups, or whatever. She always had been hurt in the past. Back to when she was a teenager and fat. Even now with her new figure the feeling never went away, that sense of inadequacy. Her body was decent and almost as curvy as Ronnie's, though she stood a couple of inches taller. If only she had Ronnie's beauty.

But she didn't, she would have to make do. *Irish*. No chance he'd be Daniel Day-Lewis in *The Last of the Mohicans*? Irish boy probably was tall, skinny, red haired, and freckled with an Adam's apple that bobbed like a top every time he drew breath. No doubt looked like the cartoon guy from the Lucky Charms cereal commercials. She glanced at her friend.

"Is this important to you? That I go?"

Ronnie held her mug between her hands rubbing them back and forth as if to draw the warmth from it.

"Like you said, Nick's not going to make this easy. He wants to see me, but it seems he doesn't want to be alone with me. Julie, I don't know what to make of him. He's so closed off. Yet—"

"Well don't leave me hanging, what?" Julie demanded.

"He's an amazingly tender lover, but he is also wild and feral and I love it. I told you he came over to see how I was doing after Tyler had been shot?" Julie nodded. "He was so gentle and kind. I almost melted at his feet right then and there. Then the next time he became distant and cool. I can't figure it out."

"The man obviously has walls up. I know you said his past wasn't great. Sounds like he has emotional issues," Julie replied.

"Join the club."

"It's a big membership. I'm a card-carrying member myself. Look Ronnie, you have to decide what you want from Nick. If it's just great, mind-numbing, soul-stirring sex, then take what you want and move on. If it's more than that, you have to find a way to tear down the walls between you. Listen to me, Dr. Phil over here," she chuckled softly, "Like I'm one to give advice." She shrugged. "I'll go with you on this drink thing Saturday night with Shamrock Boy. But don't you dare slip off with Nick and leave me alone with this guy!"

Ronnie reached over and hugged her tight.

"I'm glad we hooked back up, I so need a friend right now. Thank you, I'll call Nick. How bad can it be?"

Ronnie almost skipped into the back room to make her call. Julie shook her head. Ronnie had it bad. She just didn't know it yet. She took another sip of tea. Her stomach rolled. A blind date. *Wonderful.*

Chapter Fourteen

Saturday night arrived quickly enough, and Julie did nothing but fret for hours. What to wear, how to style her shoulder-length hair, and sitting now in the White Owl Pub with Ronnie, she tried to keep her hands from trembling. First, she hated these damned pubs and bars that insisted on having these high stools you had to perch yourself on like a young robin nervous at the thought of flying south. Damn, she sat so high off the ground she was in nose-bleed territory here. At least she and Ronnie faced the entrance.

She kept glancing every few minutes for the arrival of the men. Why she was flustered she'd no idea. It wasn't as if this was a *serious* date, her and Celtic Boy were here as buffers only. Actually, they were being used to an extent, but for a good cause. Julie had to admit she was curious to see Nick Crocetti up close and personal, how he acts and reacts around Ronnie. The only time she'd seen him was in full Terminator mode riding around on his big-ass motorcycle, usually scowling. Well, there was that time in the parking lot he was shirtless and washing his bike. She could've sold tickets. Stunning chest and muscles on display. Reaching for the long-stemmed wineglass, Julie took a sip of the Riesling.

The two men walked through the door. You could've heard a collective gasp throughout the pub that seemed to be filled mostly by women. Never had Julie seen such a pair of glorious bookends. Neither did all the females in the pub, it seemed.

Nick Crocetti was even better looking up close. Tonight he did not appear in full Terminator mode, but wore tight, black jeans and black sneakers and a white sweater that accentuated his golden, dusky skin. He smiled and talked to his friend. Nick was utterly stunning and ruggedly handsome.

Nothing however, prepared Julie for the sight of Lorcan Byrne. He was in a word—beautiful. He had those classic handsome looks that are rarely seen on a man except in a cologne ad in a magazine. Yet, he didn't have any of the femininity some of those men possessed. Julie's insides roiled and fluttered. She felt entirely inadequate. If she could've scrambled down off the damned stool she would've run for the back door and headed home. A vision of him running through the woods shirtless and carrying a musket with that long, thick, glorious hair rippling behind him—which was longer than hers by the way—ran through her mind. Yep. Daniel Day-Lewis in *The Last of the Mohicans*, only—better.

He smiled in return to whatever Nick said. Oh, dear god, he had dimples: deeply carved dimples on either side of a full, generous, sensual mouth. She glanced away. It hurt to look at him. This was the type of man she would never, ever have and it tore at her heart. She wished now he did resemble the animated guy from the Lucky Charms commercial, it would've made it far more bearable. Oh, why couldn't he be some wizened leprechaun?

"I can't," she murmured to Ronnie who waved to Nick.

"What did you say, Julie?"

"I can't do this, look at him. I have to go."

Julie tried to get down off the stool, but Ronnie grabbed her arm firmly.

"You're staying right here. I know what you're thinking, Julie. You think he's too good-looking for you. Don't you dare think that! You're better than any woman in this room," Ronnie said.

Julie felt beads of sweat pop out at her hairline. Oh yeah, that would be attractive. She managed a quick glance as they were almost to the table. Byrne's eyes were large and framed by thick lashes. Under the shimmering lights, she could see red highlights in his walnut-brown hair. Beautiful.

She couldn't quite make out the color of his eyes, hard to tell under these illuminations, but a blue-green combination she'd never seen before. Suddenly, those lamps of his were fixed on her and she swallowed hard. She could imagine what he thought; *she's a mongrel, sitting next to the best in show.*

Next to Ronnie she felt like a shabby, unwanted mutt. Taking another sip of wine, she watched the men over the rim. Nick placed a kiss on Ronnie's cheek. Nick turned and held out his hand to her, it was large with long, elegant fingers.

"You must be Julie."

She took it. His hand was warm and masculine. He let go, and he and Lorcan took seats opposite them.

"Julie, Ronnie, this is my friend, Lorcan Byrne. Lorcan, this is Veronica Barnes and Julie Denison."

"Pleased to meet you, ladies," Lorcan replied.

Julie had to grip the table or she would've slid off the stool into a puddle on the floor. A voice deeper than Nick's, with that wonderful, expressive, rolling, Irish brogue she thought only existed in the movies. His eyes twinkled mischievously and his smile was pure wicked sin.

He was too much of everything she ever wanted and would never have. This was heartbreaking. She toyed with the idea of dying her hair a few shades lighter or perhaps adding golden highlights to her perpetually mousy brown hair. She wished now she'd done it before tonight. He gazed at her, assessing and grading her no doubt.

Grabbing the wine glass, she threw the contents back. Reaching for the bottle, she poured some more. She needed courage and if the liquid variety was the only thing available, then hell, she was using it.

She could think of nothing to say, her voice all but dried up and closed over in her throat. Nor could she follow the conversation. The voices around her became muffled and intermixed with the music into a cacophony of unintelligible vowels and consonants. She could feel his gaze on her. Be damned if she would look at him.

"So what do you do, Lorcan?" She heard Ronnie ask over the din of pub noise.

Julie perked up. This she wanted to hear.

"I'm running a club with a mate on the outskirts of town. The Playpen."

Julie all but snorted her wine through her nose. "You're running the Bada Bing? What are you, an Irish Tony Soprano?" The table became quiet. "Ah, the Bada Bing—it was a strip club—" She tried to explain lamely.

"We had *The Sopranos* in Ireland, darlin'. I know what the Bada Bing is," Lorcan said.

Julie felt her cheeks flush in hot embarrassment. What made her blurt that out? What if he was a gangster? She took another long swig of wine. The way he said *darlin'* made her thighs sweat and her breasts tighten. *Oh please, I don't want to be attracted to this guy!*

Ronnie laid her hand on her arm gently as if telling her to slow down on throwing back the vino. Or maybe she sensed how uptight she was. Regardless, the gesture helped. Julie took a large breath, held it, and exhaled.

"Sorry, didn't mean to imply anything," she mumbled.

Lorcan sat back, his arms crossed. Julie glanced at him for the first time since he sat down. He was indeed staring, one perfect eyebrow arched as he regarded her. He wore a V-neck sweater and she could see perfectly formed pectorals lightly dusted with brown hair under the crossed arms. He must have thought her a fool, a drunken idiot. She pushed the wine glass away.

"Tony Soprano, I don't know whether to be flattered or insulted. Maybe—" he winked. "You're not far off, darlin'."

Oh, sweet god. He *was* a gangster! She saw a movie once, all about tough, cut-your-throat-for-an-insult Irish thugs. Was that what he was? Julie squirmed on the stool. For all of the sudden, that made Lorcan all the more attractive, how sick was that?

Ronnie grabbed her purse. "I'm just going to go to the washroom."

Nick stood as well. "Yeah, me too."

*

Lorcan glanced at the woman across from him. She stared into the depths of her wineglass. As if she couldn't bear to look at him for some reason. She was certainly knocking back the wine. He wondered if she even spoke until she made the Bada Bing comment. Actually, Lorcan found it funny. He had the feeling she was quite witty and intelligent. She was not a beauty mind you, but Lorcan didn't put much stock in a person's looks.

He certainly squired quite a few lovely ladies in the last few years and bedded them as well. However, he didn't discriminate. If a plain girl charmed him—he bedded her, too. He cocked his head and assessed Julie. She wasn't that plain. In fact, he thought her cute. Lorcan's gaze raked over her torso. A full bust, always a plus. Lorcan stood, grabbed his beer, and sat next to her. He heard her intake of breath. He gazed at the rest of her body. Very lovely, curves a man could happily get lost in.

"You've known Veronica since school then, Nick too, I assume?" he smiled.

He leaned in close so she had no escape. Inhaling, her alluring scent was a mixture of fresh air and freshly baked bread: a very enticing mix.

"You could say that. Not Nick, though. Not really. Nick doesn't let anyone close, even back then," Julie replied.

Her eyes were a lovely mixture of hazel and gold. She really had the loveliest skin.

"Aye, I got that about him."

"So why you?" Julie asked.

"Could be my Irish charm, works on the lads as well as the lasses. Though I don't seem to be doing so well with you."

Lorcan cupped her cheek. She gasped at the contact and so did he. An electric bolt of intense heat roared up his arm from the touch of her soft skin. *Bloody hell!* He drew back his hand like he'd been burned. Julie stared at him, confusion clear on her face. Lorcan stood, reached for his beer, and returned to his original seat. Bewilderment washed over him. Veronica and Nick reappeared, both looking a little flushed. Lorcan imagined they had a quick snog, he could sense the vibes.

Veronica leaned in and whispered to Julie, "What is it? What's the matter?"

"Nothing—I want to go home," she said.

Veronica patted Julie's hand and whispered something to her Lorcan could not hear. The DJ announced they were open for karaoke for the next hour. Lorcan's eyebrow rose. His touch was that upsetting she wanted to go home?

Veronica clasped her hands together. "Oh, Nick! I always wanted to hear you sing."

Nick laughed. "I can't sing worth a damn."

"Nobody can that gets up on stage, but I would like to see you try," she purred seductively.

Nick snorted. "I don't think so."

"I double dog dare you," she teased.

"Oh? And what will I get if I sing?"

Veronica stood and whispered in his ear. Nick's eyes widened. Lorcan could well imagine what the lass suggested.

"Done, baby. You're on."

Veronica giggled and clapped.

"But I'm picking the song," Nick said.

"Why don't you pick *Bad to the Bone*?" Julie snickered. "Wasn't that in the *Terminator 2* movie?"

Veronica hit Julie on the arm. "Julie!"

Lorcan threw back his head and laughed. The lass *was* funny, how enchanting. He got the Terminator reference. It fit Nick, especially when he was decked out in his motorcycle leather.

Nick shook his head, and didn't respond to the Terminator remark. "No, I've something in mind. I'll go see if they have it."

Lorcan stood. "I'll come with you, mate."

*

After the men left, Veronica turned to Julie. "Are you okay? Did this Lorcan say something to upset you?"

"No, he didn't say anything. Ronnie, can we please go after the karaoke?" she almost pleaded.

"Oh Julie, you're attracted to him."

"Who wouldn't be? Look at him!" Her arm waved toward the stage area where he and Nick flipped through a binder.

Veronica gave her a quick hug. "I'll see if we can leave after Nick is finished."

Veronica patted her arm and glanced toward the stage. Julie was right: Lorcan Byrne was incredibly handsome. He had perfect features and the type of tall, slim, musculature that universally appealed. No doubt had a trail of women after him. Her gaze scanned around the pub. In fact, both Nick and Lorcan were receiving a lot of stares and open lustful looks from quite a few women. A slight stab of jealousy picked at Veronica. Maybe Nick performing on stage wasn't a good idea. Actually, she was shocked Nick agreed, of course, for what she promised most men would jump through fiery hoops while balancing plates on their fingers.

Nick kept to himself, but he obviously wasn't shy. Thinking of his impromptu strip tease brought a smile to her face. Nope, not shy at all.

Veronica glanced at Julie: the poor woman really was upset by this double date thing. Lorcan Byrne personified the Irish hunk in spades. How did he and Nick become friends? Nick didn't have friends, never did as far as she knew. This was a fascinating development. There was a whole side of Nick she'd no idea existed.

Lorcan walked back to the table and sat on the nearby stool. "He's going to bloody well do it. This should be interesting." Lorcan took a swig of beer. "He wants to go first, get it over with. Shite, he has more guts than I do."

"What song did he pick? Probably classic rock," Veronica reasoned.

Lorcan winked. "It's a surprise. Wish I'd brought my camera. Wait, did either of you lasses bring your mobile—I mean—cell phone? I can take snaps with that. Left mine at the club."

Veronica retrieved hers from her purse and after showing Lorcan how to use it, he turned on his stool to face the front of the pub.

Sure enough, Nick approached the stage. Climbing the stairs, he walked to the monitor and reached for the microphone. A table of six women in front giggled and jumped up and down in their seats. Veronica rolled her eyes. *Oh, Please.*

The opening staccato beat of *Bad Case of Loving You* filled the pub, Nick growled 'Whoa' with a vibrant baritone. The women sitting at the front table went wild as did every other female in the place. Veronica groaned. Maybe she should've had him do this for her in private, now she had to share this with every salivating woman in the room. Lorcan laughed and snapped pictures of the display.

Nick got right into it. His slim hips thrust in time to the beat and his package was on full display. Veronica could swear a spotlight shined directly on his crotch. He sang the chorus and the pub erupted. His face and chest now glistened with beads of sweat from the almost sexual exertion and heat only partly caused by the hot lights. Veronica glanced around, women young and old of every shape and size were on their feet, squealing like fan-girls.

One woman in the back screamed, "Take your shirt off!"

What amazed Veronica is Nick could sing. Well, she figured he could sing with that glorious, sexy voice of his, but she didn't realize just how well he would do on stage. The man had a presence. He had every cadence and growl of Robert Palmer's down cold. He wasn't even looking at the monitor. He knew the lyrics by heart.

Nick slid into the chorus again then lifted his head and looked straight at her. Her heart lurched and rolled. The sensual look he gave her sent all the women into a kind of frenzy. The women at the front table were now on their feet and in front of the stage like rock groupies. She wouldn't be surprised to see a pair of thongs hit Nick square in the face.

Nick sang about liking it on top. He pointed right at her. Every pair of eyes in the place turned and looked at her, even Julie and Lorcan. She flushed straight from her toes, how dare he? She did like it on top and Nick knew it. God, she was mortified. More women gathered in front of him. He continued with the rest of the song, he lifted part of his sweater halfway up his chest and the women squealed. Veronica couldn't believe this. Nick's blatant sexuality, his damned virile maleness, was on full display and he reveled in it. This turned out to be the longest three minutes in her life.

The enjoyment of his performance slowly seeped away. After the heated groping in the hallway when they headed to the restrooms and his deep, passionate kisses, she ached to see Nick perform. Foolish of her to think she'd be the only one to notice his rugged appeal. Finally, mercifully, the song ended.

The pub erupted into a cacophony of applause, wolf whistles, and screams. Nick's performance was awesome. He bowed, drinking in the love and approval. He jumped off the stage and the nearby group of women surrounded him and grabbed his arms. They gazed up at him admiringly.

One willowy, tall blonde thrust a piece of paper into his hand. Nick made his way back to their table, but the women wouldn't let him, they chattered like magpies and gazed at him like he was the second coming. Veronica felt the rage building. You'd think he was a rock star after a concert instead of karaoke.

Nick tried to detach himself from the ladies. Finally, he sauntered back to the table unaided. Veronica was sure her color changed from deep-red to pea-green. Envy, she felt it and drowned in it. Those women touched Nick, admired Nick, and she wanted to gouge out their eyes with rusty spoons.

He sat back down on the stool, taking a long, leisurely pull on his bottle of beer. His chest heaved; rivers of sweat flowed down his face and matted his hair. Lorcan smiled and patted him on the back. Nick's amber eyes glittered with vibrant life.

"What's that?" she snapped a little more tersely than she had meant to.

Nick looked at the piece of paper. "Oh, nothing."

He crammed it into the front pocket of his tight jeans. Veronica saw it. That bimbo's phone number and he kept it. Suddenly, she felt as lousy as Julie looked. For all his passionate kisses, he'd never be able to stay faithful or committed, and it tore at her heart. As appealing as Nick could be on so many levels, there was much about him that was heartbreaking. How could she be with a man who didn't want any kind of permanence, even a thinly veiled one? She realized with stark clarity she wanted a man who could stay faithful; because he cared. Respected her, and hell, maybe even loved her. Veronica glanced at Nick. He and Lorcan were laughing at the pictures. Lorcan handed the phone back to her and she stuffed it in her purse without looking at the shots.

The sickening feeling stabbed deep, Nick was not the man she truly wanted. When did she become so hopelessly old-fashioned? A man with honor, why was it so damned hard to find one?

Veronica stood suddenly. "We have to go."

Nick's eyebrows knotted in confusion. "What? Why? You haven't even finished your wine."

Veronica grabbed the wineglass and downed it all in one swallow. She slammed it back on the table almost shattering it.

"There. Done."

Nick stood and pulled her away.

"Excuse us." When they were far enough from the table, Nick said, "What's going on? I thought you were coming back to my place tonight?"

The temptation to goad him and to tell him to call the blonde bimbo was hard to resist. The words dissolved on her tongue. He might do it to spite her and the thought of Nick's muscular body writhing on top of any other woman shattered her heart. She was falling for him. She knew it. She was going to be hurt.

Big time.

Thinking back, it started on that first date when he pulled the candles and wine out of the picnic basket. Then the rose, that perfect, red rose.

Someone on stage warbled a Journey ballad, slaughtering it in fact. Blinking back the tears she refused to shed, she said as calmly as she could, "Julie's upset. I should be with her."

Nick glanced back at Julie sitting with her head down. Lorcan simply stared at Julie with a confused look on his face.

"Why? Did something happen? Did I miss something?"

"I don't know, so I'd better find out."

"Okay, well, why not come for supper tomorrow night instead?"

Damn him! She struggled to find an excuse, but his warm, beer-laced breath fanned her cheeks as he leaned down and whispered in her ear, "I have a couple of T-bone steaks and an indoor grill, a bottle of red wine; I also have a surprise for you. Say you'll come."

His voice was deep, seductive, and impossible to refuse. Her panties were soaking wet just from his nearness and that husky, come hither voice. He could sit and recite the phone book and she could sit and listen, enraptured by the cadence of it.

"I thought you were working tomorrow," she replied rather coolly.

"Only until four o'clock, then Kevin takes over. Come on, say you'll come."

Her head spun. The rapid influx of the wine she supposed.

"Okay, I'll be there." She walked away from him. "Julie, let's go."

Lorcan stood and walked over to Julie, took her hand, and laid a brief kiss on it.

"It was delightful to meet you, Julie, darlin'."

She pulled her hand out of his grasp, turned, and fled out the front door without saying a word. Lorcan genuinely looked puzzled.

"She's not feeling well. I'd better get her home. Sorry to cut the evening short. Nice to meet you, Lorcan."

She followed Julie straight out the front door. Standing on the sidewalk she glanced around, where did Julie go? Then she heard it, quiet sniffling. Julie stood around the side of the building shadowed in darkness. Veronica's heart broke. She never would've suggested this get-together if she knew her friend was going to be hurt like this. Veronica stepped into the darkness.

"What is it, Julie? Did he say something? Please, talk to me!"

Julie exhaled shakily. "I usually don't go to pieces like this, really I don't. But it's been so long since I've been in the company of a man. It brought it all back. High school dances, blind dates, the teasing and the hurtful remarks. All I could see was my former fat self sitting on the sidelines, watching others having fun, watching them laugh behind their hands. The most popular boy would ask me for a dance because he lost a bet and had to dance with the fat girl." She cleared her throat to control her emotions. "That's what it felt like. He looked at me and talked to me because he had to. I was that fat, sad girl again. Maybe I always will be deep inside."

Veronica hugged her friend close. "Oh Julie, I never should've suggested it. He affected you, didn't he?"

"Yes, he did. He tried to talk to me while you guys were gone. He touched my cheek. His touch felt wonderful, but Lorcan couldn't wait to get away from me. Then I made those stupid comments. I felt sixteen all over again."

"Come on, I have a dozen peanut butter cookies with our names on them plus a bottle of white wine. Let's go drown our sorrows."

"Oh no, Ronnie, you too?"

Veronica put her arm through Julie's and headed toward the parking lot.

"Yes, me too."

*

Nick sat, stunned. What in hell just happened? At least she was coming over to dinner. The evening just plunged into a deep freeze and he had no idea why.

Lorcan leaned toward him "You mind explaining what just happened here, mate?"

Nick shook his head. "I've no damned idea. What happened with you and Julie?"

"I wish I knew. Guess I offended her in some way. She acted like I was not worth the shite you would scrape off your shoe. Too bad, I kind of liked her." Lorcan stood and waved to a waiter. "More drinks, mate. We both could use them."

Chapter Fifteen

Nick unlocked the door of his bar around noon Sunday. He and Lorcan stayed awhile at the White Owl the previous night, had a few beers, then left. A few women stopped by the table, tried to buy them drinks and engage them in flirtatious conversation, but neither Nick nor Lorcan had been in the mood. Both of them could have gone home with the pick of the litter quite easily. Though Lorcan didn't brag, Nick had the feeling he indulged in female company as eagerly as he did. *Lorcan kind of liked Julie?* She didn't seem his type, not that he really knew what Lorcan's type was.

Nick shook his head. He didn't like the way she treated Lorcan, what did he say? *'Like shite on the bottom of a shoe.'* Guess Nick felt a little protective of his new and only friend. Nick glanced up, a black Crown Victoria pulled into the parking lot and a tall man with tousled blond hair climbed out of the car. Cop. He radiated the aura. The way he stood, the way he walked, and the Crown Vic were a dead giveaway. Nick squinted. Not just any cop, Tyler Barnes, Ronnie's brother. Nick curled his lip, probably come to threaten him or warn him away from Ronnie.

An older man walked into the bar and took a seat on a nearby stool. Nick headed straight for the Bunn coffee machine, poured a mug, and placed it in front of the man with a spoon, napkin, and two creamers.

"Same Frank? Whisky shot as well?"

"Yes, Nick. Thank you," the soft-spoken man replied.

Tyler walked through the door and right up to the bar.

"I'm Veronica Barnes's brother. I want a word."

Nick's mouth quirked, talked like a cop, too. Nick motioned to a table.

"I'll join you in a minute."

Nick reached for a double shot glass and nimbly poured two fingers of whisky, sliding the glass toward Frank without spilling a drop.

Reaching for two white coffee mugs from under the counter, he poured, and carried them to the table.

"Cream? Sugar?" Nick asked.

"No, just black."

Nick sat opposite him. He remembered Tyler from school. The golden god had been popular, head of the student union and on the football team. He had girls trailing behind him, other guys, too. It was funny that Tyler ended up being a cop. Nick thought he heard he got a scholarship to some Ivy League school. *Guess he didn't go.*

"So, is this the big scene where you warn me off your sister? A few subtle threats? Lean on me and my small bar? Yeah, this is a real hotbed of criminal activity." Nick swept his arm around. "And there is a real criminal type there, Frank Coffey. Do you remember him, Barnes? He taught chemistry at Rockland High."

Tyler's gaze turned toward the cheerless looking man at the bar, hunched over his coffee and whisky chaser. "Yeah, I had Mr. Coffey. What is he, a barfly now?"

Nick took a sip of the coffee. "He comes in every Sunday after visiting his wife's grave. He's no barfly, just a lonely old man who misses his wife. No other family to speak of, he comes in here for coffee, a few drinks, and conversation. He's led quite an interesting life. Did you know he served in Vietnam? Decorated, two Purple Hearts, a Bronze Star, and the Legion of Merit. He carries shrapnel in his leg to this day."

"I'd no idea—he told you all this?"

Nick shrugged. "I'm a bartender. I hear a lot of stories. I listen. I don't judge. I keep their glass filled."

"The hallmarks of a good bartender."

"I'd like to think so. Are you here to impart some hard-luck story, some tragic love affair, or is it to warn me off your sister?"

Tyler shifted uncomfortably in his chair. "Not to warn exactly. Maybe find out your intentions."

Nick laughed. "Intentions? What is this, the fifties?"

Tyler's eyes narrowed. "This isn't funny. I love my sister. I don't want her to get hurt. I don't want her to be another scalp hanging on your belt."

Nick sat back in his chair and folded his arms across his chest. He tried to hide his anger as he studied Barnes. The temptation to land a fist in that cop face of his—appealed. *Scalp. On his belt.* Nick remained silent. Seething inwardly, he tried to regain control of his emotions.

"You've a reputation, Crocetti," Tyler continued. "Even back in high school, I heard you did all the girls in 12B. And you've been busy ever since, racked up quite an impressive count. I don't want my sister tossed in the recycle bin with the rest of the women."

Nick snorted. "All the girls in 12B? Jesus, I didn't have sex with any girls in 12B. I don't know how that rumor got started."

Tyler took a sip of coffee. "I also heard about Miss McGregor. You were the envy of every guy in the senior class. The hot, young teacher? Was that just gossip too?"

"I thought you were here to talk about your sister, not a half-assed high school rumor," Nick snapped.

"I'm just establishing your well-earned reputation here."

"Okay, then. The rumor's true about Darla McGregor. I was of legal age. I thought I was in love. She tossed me to the curb. I was crushed as only an eighteen-year-old would be with an intense, first love. Happy now? Is that what you wanted to hear?" Nick said.

"What are your feelings for my sister, then?"

"I don't know and even if I did I wouldn't tell you. It's none of your damned business."

Tyler rubbed the back of his neck, his demeanor and voice softened.

"Look, Ronnie's been through a lot the last couple of years, starting with our father's death. She took it pretty hard. Then the short marriage to William Titus ..."

"Ronnie told me about it. I know she was hurt," Nick interrupted.

"I don't think even she realizes how deep the hurt runs. I'm glad she moved back home, I've really missed her. This bakery is a real gamble. I hope to hell it works out for her. But if you just plan on having some quick affair with her and moving on, I'd rather you broke it off with her now before it goes any deeper. That's all I'm saying. Don't. Fucking. Hurt. Her."

Nick listened to the passionately spoken words. Tyler's concern for Ronnie reverberated in his tone of voice. As annoyed as he felt by Tyler's interference in something Nick himself did not even have a handle on, he could understand it.

"We've only been seeing each other a couple of weeks. I've no idea where this is going, let alone how I feel. I promise you, I won't hurt her. That is the last thing I want to do. I've been honest with your sister so I'll be honest with you. I'll let her down gently should it come to that. I'm not going into detail about what is going on between Ronnie and me. It's private."

Tyler nodded. "Fair enough. You're right. It's really none of my business. Just chalk it up to a concerned brother who loves his sister. She is also my friend and always has been since we were kids."

Nick stood. "Barnes, bring your coffee over to the bar. Let's keep Frank company. I'll bet he remembers you. If you've got time, I think he'd appreciate you saying hello and listening to a story or two of his while you finish your coffee."

"All right. Sure, why not?"

*

Veronica struggled all day whether to go to Nick's or call him and cancel, but ultimately, she decided to go. Driving toward Nick's, her mind raced.

Sleep did not come easy last night, all she could picture was Nick having sex with that blonde skank who shoved her phone number in his sweaty hand, the number he stuck in his jeans pocket. What right did she have to seethe all night? He said he wasn't committed, but would try. Just how hard was he willing to try? Bottom line, she didn't want to share him—with anyone. And that realization had her awake and looking wide-eyed at the stucco ceiling at three in the morning. Only seeing each other a couple of weeks and already she staked a claim? *Big mistake.*

Midnight confessions be damned, she was starting to have feelings for Nick Crocetti. Deep feelings. She knew if she continued to see him they'd grow deeper. That night in his bed and his arms was beyond anything she had ever experienced before. She wanted more. She wanted him.

While his virile, masculine body and beyond earthly lovemaking skills appealed, something about Nick touched her deeply. In a place no other man ever reached before, not even William Titus. She could love him. Easily. Maybe she was part way there already.

Veronica turned onto Prince William Street toward the dock area. Play it cool, stay for supper, then leave. Right. Sounds like a plan. She wouldn't wind up in his bed this night. She moaned aloud thinking of Nick slamming into her, his head thrown back roaring his release, the cords in his neck straining, the vein on his forehead prominent and pulsating. The guttural, animal growls as he pounded into her. He was not quiet and neither was she. Veronica loved it.

Hell, if he so much as kissed her with those sensual lips she would go to his bed willingly, do whatever he wanted for as long as he wanted. He was a sexual pied piper.

She pulled in around back and parked behind the bar so she could use Nick's private entrance. *Stay cool. Polite ... but cool. In control.*

Smoothing her skirt, she stepped out of her car. Nevertheless, she took great pains in her appearance today. The outfit consisted of a tight, sexy black skirt and a dressy, gold cotton shirt. She even bought a black garter belt and hose with matching bra and thong as Nick seemed to like that. She felt incredibly feminine and sexy. High heel black pumps completed the look. She wondered now if she should've worn her sweats and Orioles t-shirt, this outfit could be sending the wrong message. *Take me against the wall and ravish me.* Is that what she wanted? The look didn't exactly fit her trying to stay cool and detached. She rang the bell.

Heavy footsteps descended the stairs from the above apartment. Her heart fluttered in anticipation. Nick opened the door. A butcher's block apron was tied loosely around his hips and he wiped his hands on a dishtowel. His face appeared flushed from presiding over a hot stove. He wore a tight, sleeveless t-shirt tucked into a pair of black khakis.

"Come in." He looked her up and down. "Damn," he whistled huskily. "You look fantastic."

He sprinted up the stairs ahead of her. Oh my, she had only ever seen him in leather pants or jeans, but the khakis hugged his muscular, taut ass like a second skin.

"I have to get back to my potato skins!" he yelled as he disappeared around the corner.

She slowly followed him up the narrow stairs. Stilettos hindered her going any faster. Laying her purse by the front door, she walked into his small kitchen. The odor of fresh green onions and cooked bacon inundated her senses.

"Nick! Potato skins? Aren't they a lot of work?"

Veronica glanced at the cookie sheet with the little potato boats on them. Clustered in each one was finely chopped green onion, little bits of cut-up cooked bacon, and shredded cheese. She *adored* potato skins, how did he know? She only had them a few times a year, they were sinfully fattening, a heart attack on a plate.

"Yeah, but it's worth it. I baked the potatoes last night."

He came home from the pub—and baked potatoes? He didn't call the blonde bimbo? She almost wanted to blubber with relief.

"I went to that all-night market over on Sydney Street and bought the ingredients. Put the potatoes in to bake last night while I watched a movie. That's the key, let them cool overnight." Nick reached for a small glass measuring cup and began to drizzle the skins. "This is another little touch of mine. A little bacon grease over the top, just a little, soaks right into the potato."

Veronica couldn't believe it. While she tossed and turned and fumed all night thinking Nick was having hot, untamed sex with the slut, he'd been home watching a movie and baking potatoes. Her plan of staying cool and detached just flew straight out the window. She wanted to throw herself in his arms and sob uncontrollably into that muscled chest. He was adorable. *Stunning, gorgeous, magnificent man.*

Nick chattered away, she never heard him talk so much. This must be the surprise he talked about, the potato skins.

"Can you get the white wine out of the fridge? And the sour cream, too. I made sure I bought the real deal, none of that low fat, fat free, watery stuff. I got the thickest, tangiest sour cream I could find." He stood up straight suddenly and turned to look at her. "You do like potato skins, I hope."

Veronica opened the fridge and reached for the wine and sour cream and laid them on the counter.

"Nick, I love them. I can't think of anything better."

"The steaks are marinating. And I made a salad. Hope that's enough."

Veronica stroked his smooth, freshly shaved cheek. His Nautica Aftershave mixed with the musky, masculine scent that was Nick's alone. So alluring.

"Nick, it's perfect," she whispered.

"Did I tell you how beautiful you look?"

"You did. Thanks."

"I'll go change my shirt when I finish cooking. This old sleeveless t-shirt is best, cooler for cooking that is."

Veronica raised her hand to stroke his chest. The muscles were clearly visible through the shirt. They bunched and flexed under her touch.

"Don't bother on my account," she purred.

"Damn—"

Nick gave her a deep, thorough, and passionate kiss. Veronica threw her arms around his neck and kissed him right back. She wrapped one leg around him as best as she was able with the tight skirt and pulled him closer. He cupped her ass, lifted, and brought her in against his hardening cock. As soon as she made contact with his potent erection, Nick stepped back.

"Ah, we'd better eat first."

Veronica staggered a bit from the abrupt release from his hot embrace. Her lips were swollen from his aggressive, sexy assault. Food? Who could think about food? Nick placed the tray of potato skins in the oven.

"Eight minutes, just enough to heat them up and melt the cheese."

Veronica could relate. She was a little heated up and melted herself. She was shredded cheese. Couldn't they have quick, eight-minute sex? No, not with Nick. Quick sex did not exist as far as Nick was concerned. The temptation to come up behind him and grab that throbbing hardness in her hands caused her mouth to go dry. He opened the wine, poured her a glass, and passed it to her.

"You're not having any?"

"No, I need something stronger."

He laid his hand lightly on the small of her back and led her out of the kitchen into his living room. He walked to his bar caddy and poured what appeared to be a whisky. He joined her on the sofa. Veronica smiled; he had kept the apron on.

"What happened last night?" Nick asked suddenly. "You flew out of there like your cute little ass was on fire. Same with your friend, Julie. Lorcan was certainly confused. So was I."

Veronica glanced down into her wine. She wasn't going to lie. Nick was always honest with her; she could at least reciprocate.

"I saw you put the phone number in your jeans pocket," she murmured.

Nick stood and marched into another room. He brought back a wastebasket.

"Here it is. I never even looked at it." He thrust the can toward her. "Have a look. It's that torn and crumpled ball of paper under the Kleenex."

Veronica flushed in embarrassment. "I don't have to look. I've no right, it just—hurt. The blonde woman was gorgeous."

Nick sat next to her. He put his arm around her shoulders.

"I already have a gorgeous blonde."

She gazed up at him. The look he gave her was entirely sincere. His eyes reflected enticing warmth, she could see clear to his soul. Oh, dear god. It happened. She *had* fallen in love with him. Oh, *how* did it happen? She's been so careful—or so she thought. He could never know. She would have to keep the feelings hidden and protected.

"I've no claim on you, Nick. You can call her or any other woman if you want." *Oh, please don't.* She knew it would rip her heart out if he started seeing another woman.

He placed his drink on the coffee table.

"Maybe I don't want to call any other women."

"What are you saying, Nick?"

Her heart leapt in her chest. The buzzer went off on the oven. Nick jumped up and sprinted toward the kitchen. Veronica moaned in frustration. What was he about to say?

Chapter Sixteen

Nick made his escape. *Pull back boy, don't go off the relationship cliff with the rest of the lemmings.* Nick grabbed the oven mitt and removed the tray of skins. The cheese bubbled and sizzled. They were done perfectly. Ever since Tyler Barnes dropped by earlier, he thought of nothing else but their discussion on relationships. What did he want with Ronnie? He had never gone through this much trouble for a woman. Talk about the height of intimacy. He never cooked a meal for a woman before either. He was giving something of himself here, something he'd never done before with anyone. Yet, he'd let both Lorcan and Ronnie close, almost at the same time. Did it mean he was ready for some kind of undeviating relationships in his life at last?

Christ, his head hurt. He hated overanalyzing anything, feelings and emotions worst of all. He reached into the cupboard for two small plates. Using tongs, he put four skins on each plate and then placed a huge dollop of sour cream on the side. Opening his cutlery drawer, he reached for two small forks. He knew as soon as he returned to the living room, Ronnie would want him to answer her question. What does he say? What harm would it do to make some sort of thin noncommittal commitment? He had done that already the other morning, didn't he?

He laid his hands on the counter and lowered his head. The fact he took that woman's phone number and tossed it in the trash without even looking at it spoke volumes. Any other time he would've called. Hell, he would have gone home with her right then and there. Had sex with her and then left.

He didn't want that kind of blasé, causal thing with Ronnie. The wild sex behind her bakery was just a taste—an appetizer. Her staying in his bed, wrapped around his body all night with him deep inside her very core was the main course. Tonight, he wanted dessert. Would that get her out of his system? Somehow he doubted it. He'd want more.

Nick always figured women were like a buffet, all different dishes, all ready to be tasted. He certainly had a variety. Was he ready for a more stable menu? He honestly didn't know. He couldn't imagine being with one woman for the rest of his life. Yet, people did it. What did he know about it? Nothing at all.

Carrying the plates, he entered the living room and handed one to her. "After we have these, I'll go put the steaks on."

He sat next to her, but not as close as before. She didn't speak, just cut into the crusty skins and lifted the fork to her mouth.

"Oh, Nick, these are delicious. How did you get the skins so crispy?"

"I brush them with oil before I bake them."

He took a bite. He had to admit they turned out pretty good. America's *The Complete Greatest Hits* played softly in the background on his classic Marantz stereo.

"Nick, you could have your own cooking show. I know the ladies would tune in. You created quite a stir at the pub last night," she laughed gently. "I'll admit I was a little jealous. All those women on their feet, cheering."

"Jeering, more like. Guess I'm more of an exhibitionist than I thought. Did you like the song?" he smiled.

"Do you?" she whispered.

"Do I what?"

"Have a bad case of loving me? Do you need to see a doctor?" She smiled, her eyes twinkling behind her glasses.

Nick almost choked on his potato skin. He walked into that one. She gave it to him with both barrels square in the chest. Ronnie laughed that husky, deep, throaty laugh that made his cock stand at attention.

"You don't have to answer that, I'm teasing. I did like the song. You can sing, Nick. I pretended you were singing only to me."

"I was singing just to you. To me, there were no other women in the room."

Nick spoke the truth. For all the women screaming in front of him, thrusting phone numbers in his hand or whispering that he meet them out back for a quickie behind the pub, he only saw Ronnie. Wanted only her. *Damn.*

She lowered her head and her glasses slid down her nose. He reached over and gently pushed them back up, then let his fingers trail down her cheek. Cupping her chin, he lifted it. Tears shimmered in her eyes.

"I don't know where this is going, Ronnie. I've never been in a relationship of any worth with a woman before. I guess what I'm saying and was trying to say the other morning is that I want us to see each other. Take things slow. You make me want to try and be faithful. No other woman has made me even consider it. That's all I can manage right now, are you okay with that?"

She nodded. "I don't want to overwhelm you, Nick, or make demands. To be honest, I'm not sure myself what I want. Going slow is fine."

He leaned in and laid a feather light kiss on her lips. She tasted like bacon and green onion and she tasted like sweet, hot desire. But first, the meal.

He stood. "I'll go fire up the indoor grill. Relax and drink your wine. I'll let you know when it's ready."

A half hour later they were sitting at the table eating and talking. They found both of them liked baseball. Nick followed the Red Sox, she the Orioles. They both watched the Sunday news shows, closet political junkies once a week. His full Sunday brunch would be on the menu tomorrow, even though it would be Monday. He'd bought extra eggs just in case.

They both loved old movies and rock music, though her taste was more recent as far as the music was concerned, his more classic. She talked a little about her past, her family. Nick was silently envious. To have such a loving home where the parents and kids actually did things together and enjoyed each other's company was something completely foreign to him. All his parents did was fight and break things. He got into trouble, probably to try and get their attention. All it accomplished was they'd turn on him and scream and fight. They never beat him, but the coldness, the indifference to him and his presence, hurt worse than any thrashing. His father would disappear for long periods of time. *Off with one of his sluts,* his mother would sneer. Guess the apple didn't fall that far from the tree. Every holiday had been forced and usually ended in tears and recriminations. He didn't have one pleasant Christmas or birthday memory. Not one. Either the days-old store-bought cake was thrown across the room in anger or the pitifully decorated Christmas tree knocked over in fury. Gifts were nonexistent. One Christmas he got a couple of Hot Wheels cars—that was it. His parents spent all of three dollars on him. *Merry friggin' Christmas.* Nick told her none of this. What would be the point? When Ronnie asked about his childhood he gave generalities, not specifics. He didn't want pity, especially not hers. With the meal over, Nick cleared the plates. He held out his hand.

"It's time for your surprise."

Ronnie cocked her head. "I thought the potato skins were it?"

"No, baby. Not even close. Come with me."

*

Veronica's heart began to pound. He pushed her gently into a sitting position on the bed.

"Stay right there, I'll be back in a moment."

Minutes ticked by. Where did he go? Suddenly, the lights were turned down in the room. Glancing at the doorway, Nick stood in shadow with his hand on the dimmer switch.

"I dinna ken if ye would like this, lass. But I did it anna' way."

Her heart dropped straight to the floor. That deep, perfect, Scottish burr. Nick walked forward wearing nothing but a kilt. Her mouth went dry. If she wasn't in love with the man before, she was now. He'd ordered—*the kilt.*

But that was not all. Nick also wore those leather wrist things. He stood, his powerful legs spread and reached behind him and placed a large sword point down in front of him. His large, masculine hands gripped the pommel.

"I toyed with the idea of a wig, seeing those models on the books all have hair down to their ass." He smiled. "I went to a bookstore to check it out. You're right, the books are popular. Lots of sites online to order this stuff, too."

Stunned, absolutely stunned. He looked fantastic. She stood and let her admiring gaze slide over his stunning body … *Fantasy #1 concerning Nick* just came to life. She walked slowly toward him, her legs wobbled.

"You did all this—for me?"

"Aye, lass. I had the kilt Fed-Exed," he replied, talking in the Scottish accent again.

"Oh yes, Nick. Keeping talking like that."

Her whole body throbbed with want. Veronica's legs finally gave out and she landed on her knees in front of him.

"Ah lass, just the position I wanted ye in."

They both laughed.

Veronica reached out to grasp his muscular legs. Her fingers felt the tight muscles in his calves. She stroked and caressed his skin. She gazed up at him, the laughter stopped. He must've seen the raw desire in her eyes, for his eyes narrowed. He looked at her with a sexy, ferocious gaze.

She wanted to touch him, feel him. Closing her eyes, she traveled upward. His legs were solid and muscular and her hands disappeared under the kilt. He wore nothing underneath. She brushed by his sac and he moaned. Her eyes snapped open. Nick leaned against the wall, his head back, his eyes closed. She hadn't done this to him yet. In fact, she'd only performed oral sex on a man once before. The sword fell to the carpet.

Veronica clasped the front of the kilt and tucked it under the waistband. Nick was fully aroused. She marveled again at the thickness of him. Her finger followed the pulsating vein that snaked its way from the base to the tip of his cock. Nick shuddered. Leaning down, she darted her tongue to the underside of his sac, then trailed it slowly up to the tip.

"Sweet Jesus," Nick moaned. Before he could react further, she took as much of him in her mouth as she could. Nick almost jumped out of his skin. "Oh, god—yeessssss."

Nick held her head while his hips began to pump, a gentle, fast thrust as not to choke her. The taste of him was musky and a touch salty. She could also taste the body wash he'd no doubt used when he'd showered. Reaching for her hand, Nick placed it at the base of his cock, moving her hand in an almost twisting motion while she continued to suck and lick him.

"Yes. Just like that."

She continued the rhythm of her hand and mouth, Nick moaned loudly, and encouraged her onward. He wasn't going to—in her mouth, was he? She wasn't sure how she felt about that, before she could react and even form a sentence, Nick climaxed.

Nick grabbed her shoulders and brought her to her feet and kissed her hard, sharing the musky taste of him. She was about to crawl out of her skin. She was losing control and panting hard. Veronica fumbled with her buttons, but couldn't get them undone, so she pulled hard. Buttons flew across the room and she dropped the blouse to the floor. She unzipped her skirt and stepped out of it.

Nick's hands gripped her waist and his heated gaze trailed down her body. He shuddered as his eyes almost rolled back in his head.

"Oh hell, what you're wearing."

Veronica smiled with feminine satisfaction. The desire showing in his eyes from staring at her in the garter belt, hose, and sexy matching bra sent her right over the edge. She managed to walk the few steps over to his bed. She leaned over the end of it, her ass high in the air and rotated her hips suggestively.

"Take me, Highlander. Now. Fast. Hard."

Nick roared that from-the-toes animal snarl of his. He moved aside the thin thong and he plunged into her to the hilt. She cried out in pure ecstasy. This felt so hot and untamed. Her fantasies had come to life. *Her wild, Highlander warrior.* Grasping her hips, he pumped madly, skin slapping against skin.

Veronica was ready to fly apart. Through her sexual haze she thought of something—why it felt so damned good—Nick wasn't wearing a condom. They were both so caught up in the fantasy and the moment, they didn't think. How could she think with him pounding into her? Nick rotated his hips in such a way as he thrust it nearly drove her mad with lust. She literally screamed as she came, the feeling intense.

Nick's breathing became more ragged. Finally he roared, but not before he pulled out and she felt his warm seed on her back. He groaned.

"Don't move," he said in a ragged tone.

Nick returned a few minutes later and cleaned her back with soft tissues in slow, gentle strokes. "I'm so sorry, I don't know what happened. Guess I got carried away."

She sighed in pure sated joy. "Guess we both did."

A warm towel moved across her back. Nick wiped gently and moved lower to where she still throbbed with need. It felt so good, that warmth, the soft towel, and his gentle and caring touch.

The overwhelming need for more flooded her senses. She wanted him to pound into her again, what was wrong with her? The words were on the tip of her tongue to verbalize her wishes when Nick stood her up straight. He cupped her cheeks as he always did. She loved it.

"That won't happen again. I'm sorry, sweetheart."

That endearment alone almost made her to cry right then and there.

"No harm done. I haven't been with that many men, Nick. I'm fine. Healthy—you know."

He kissed her long and deep then drew back and gazed at her with such aching tenderness. "Unfortunately, I've been with a lot of women, but I always use condoms and I get regular tests. I'm healthy as well."

He lifted her into his arms and laid her gently on the bed.

"I'm going to explore every inch of your skin, taste, lick, and count every freckle. This could take hours. In fact, I'm sure it will. God, I love it that you're wearing this." His hand ran down the whole length of her leg. "I love the feel of pantyhose or silk stockings." His hand roved over her high heel shoe. "I love these, too. Keep them on. Just don't dig them into my back, I'm not into pain," he smiled wickedly. "Well, maybe a little."

His warm, masculine hand started the slow trail back up her leg; she shuddered from his touch. It ignited the smoldering embers into roaring flame once again.

"But this—" He touched the garter belt and hose, his eyes closed, and he moaned. "If you wore something like this every time, I would be a happy miner."

Veronica snickered. "Happy miner? What does that mean?"

He opened his eyes and spread her legs. "I'm going to dig baby, deep. Plunder and take all your ore."

Veronica laughed again. She loved this teasing in bed. It was corny, sexy and adorable. How she longed to find a man like this. She wanted him. *Forever and ever.*

"And what about the online purchase, has it arrived yet?" she teased, running her leg along his thigh.

"Sadly, no. But it's something to look forward to, isn't it—lassie?"

He slipped into the Scottish burr again.

"Oh, Nick. If you knew what you do to me when you talk that way," she breathed raggedly. He reached between her legs.

"Och, lassie, I can feel ye, its wet ye be." He lowered his head. "Let me taste ye."

His tongue moved in and out of her slit working pure magic, her back arched off the bed and she cried out in release. Nick's eyes were hooded with desire.

"Lass, it's just the beginnin'."

Hours passed, as he promised. They were either in bed, wrapped around each other, or she was on top riding her sexy, wicked bad Highlander. Or they were sitting in a chair, her facing Nick, riding him again.

Nick kept the kilt on at her insistence. They slept a little and then awoke to make love again. One time she awoke to find Nick leaning up on one elbow gazing down at her, one long finger tracing her hardened nipple. She glanced at the digital clock by his bed. 1:28 A.M. They'd been at this for hours.

"Stay tonight, Ronnie. With me."

*

He laid soft kisses on her pebbled nipple. Her response was a slow, languid moan. Never had Nick felt this way in his life. He reached over to stroke her cheek.

"Ronnie, I ... I am—"

Nick couldn't say it. The words dissolved on his tongue. He'd been so caught up in the moment and what he felt that he almost said he was falling in love with her. *No.* He swore he would never speak those words to anyone. It would make him feel like such a freak. The words turned to ash in his mouth.

"What Nick?" she asked sleepily.

"Nothing."

His lips closed over the light brown nipple, he sucked greedily. He cupped and stroked it. He loved her breasts; he couldn't get enough. She moved over him, pushing him down to lay flat on his back. She took her breast from him, pulling it from his mouth. She leaned in close and pulled the breast toward her. Her tongue flicked outward and touched her own nipple. Nick's eyes widened and his cock twitched. Jesus, that was hot. He moaned loudly. Ronnie leaned over him, her ample breasts like succulent, low hanging fruit.

"Suck them—hard," she invited.

Nick's head came off the pillow as he grabbed her breasts. He feasted and sucked. Ronnie moaned, her back arched, and she came again. He'd lost track of how many times she'd climaxed. Ronnie was passionate; he loved it. Maybe—he loved *her*.

All he knew that in all his many sexual experiences, never had he felt such satisfaction in giving a woman pleasure. He had many women that had given him oral sex before, but it had been nothing like Ronnie's lips fastened firmly on his cock. *Nothing.* She'd paid her debt, for that is what she whispered in his ear at the pub. If he got up and sang, she would give him the blowjob of his life. It certainly was that. He almost came out of his skin it was so damned intense. And to take her from behind without a condom, never lost control like that before. He always took precautions. Thankfully, he managed to think clearly enough at the end to withdraw in time.

Sex with Ronnie was better each time. He reached for a condom. He'd never before done it this many times in a twenty-four-hour period. He rolled it on his erect cock.

"Ride me again," he moaned.

With her hand on his shoulder to steady herself, she slowly lowered inch by inch.

She rode him in a familiar rhythm they'd both found. Nick slapped the side of her thigh playfully.

"Faster baby, full gallop."

Ronnie laughed. Together they came, riding the wave. All that stuff about stars bursting and fireworks going off turned out to be true.

Every muscle in Nick's body clenched as he roared his release. Intense, shattering, the whole nine yards. Ronnie collapsed on his chest in exhaustion. Both were covered in a thin sheen of sweat.

Nick tenderly kissed her forehead. "I think we should get a shower."

Ronnie yawned, snuggling in closer to him. Her hand aimlessly swirled through the hair on his chest. "You go first."

"We'll shower together."

Nick stood and walked to the window, peeking through the blind slats at the star-covered sky above. He glanced back at Ronnie, her eyes were as round as saucers.

He laughed. "Never showered with a man before?"

She shook her head briskly.

Nick moved to her side of the bed and scooped her up in his arms. She squealed as he headed toward the bathroom.

"Don't be shy with me, sweetheart. I've seen every part of your body from all angles. Every mole and freckle." He leaned down and licked a dark brown mole above her nipple. "Every vein." His tongue moved to her neck, and she shuddered with desire. "Even that small blemish on your arm."

Ronnie moaned in protest. "You aren't supposed to point out my flaws!"

"We all have them, baby. No one's perfect."

He lowered her to the floor, sitting her on the closed toilet seat. Nick leaned in to start the water in the shower. He could feel Ronnie's hot gaze on him.

"You are absolute perfection," she teased.

Nick stuck his hand under the spray waiting for the right temperature. "You're making me blush."

"I've never seen someone so comfortable in their own skin, is that a man thing? You guys have no compunctions about walking around naked, using urinals in front of other guys, using showers at the gym— women? Forget it."

Nick pulled her up and into the shower with him.

"You're starting to babble, I notice you do that when you're tired. Come here."

He pulled her close, squirted body wash onto the washcloth and began to soap her up.

She leaned back against him and sighed, her eyes were closed. When his hands passed the front of her breasts, he could feel his cock jolt and stir to life. Not again. This was unbelievable. Even though he hardened with desire, he would not initiate sex. She was too tired and probably too sore. Ronnie could barely stand up. *No more tonight.*

In the morning? A whole other ball of wax. Frankly, he was damned tired as well. After washing them both, he turned off the water and took a large, fluffy bath sheet and began to dry Ronnie off, then himself. Nick scooped her into his arms and carried her to bed. She yawned and sighed, nestling her lips into his neck.

"Nick," she said so softly he could barely hear her.

Tucking her under the sheet and blanket, he crawled in next to her and pulled her into his embrace, her head on his shoulder. She snuggled closer.

She yawned again. "I could get used to this."

She dropped off to sleep. Her soft breath feathered across his shoulder. The thing of it was—he could get used to this, too. Very easily.

Chapter Seventeen

Veronica opened one eye, she heard pounding, was it her head? She rubbed her eyes as sunlight caressed her skin. Morning, where was Nick? The pounding became louder so she turned her head toward the evasive noise. Nick sat at his computer gloriously naked and clicking away at the desktop icons. He glanced at her and smiled that wicked, sexy grin.

"Hey, sweetheart. Good morning. I thought before I cook you a huge brunch that we would maybe have a little rock sex."

Oh, she was so glad she had decided not to open her bakery until noon on Mondays. Good thing she had enough baked goods prepared to get her through the day. She could stay with Nick a few more hours. Bonus!

He turned up the volume on his speakers. She recognized the rock beat, classic rock from Golden Earring. Was she up for this? She was barely awake!

Nick stood, fully aroused. She felt herself grow wet immediately. *Guess she was up for it.*

Reaching for the near empty box of condoms by the bed, he gave her another sinful grin. Rolling one on his erection, he climbed onto the bed and balanced himself on his knees. This man had stamina beyond all she thought men were capable of. Perhaps the newness of the sex between them accounted for the frenzied activity, surely this would wear off and he would tire of her. She knew deep down she'd never tire of him.

She loved him, heart and soul. This off-the-charts physical aspect was icing on the cake. Why she fell in love with a man she barely knew for three weeks still puzzled her. Was she jumping in the deep end of the pool here as she did with William Titus? There was so much she didn't know about Nick, yet she had the feeling he shared more with her than he had with anyone before in his entire life. She wanted to know more, she wanted to heal him and to fill the loneliness she felt emanate from his very being. Perhaps he could heal the lonesomeness in her. She'd been alone for such a long time. The intimacy she shared with Nick had become the most potent and significant experience of her life. His long fingers caressed her folds. Her legs fell apart in invitation and she moaned.

"You're wet, sweetheart. Soaking, wringing wet. I love it," Nick growled seductively.

Staying on his knees, he moved between her legs. Taking a pillow, he stuffed it under her rear end to elevate her for his perfect thrust. And thrust he did, taking possession of her body to the hilt. Her back arched, she would never grow tired of the way he filled and stretched her.

Almost immediately, Nick's hips began to thrust against her in perfect symmetry to the pounding rock beat of the song.

"Let the beat of the music take over your senses," he purred.

She laid her head back and closed her eyes doing exactly as Nick suggested. His muscular, slim hips were relentless. His deep, sensuous voice began to sing along, something about the twilight zone. She felt as if she floated in that zone. Nick had taken her to another plane, another planet, more than once. She could feel her orgasm building. She panted and moaned loudly.

"Come for me, sweetheart, fly apart for me." He didn't miss a beat. *Rock sex.*

Oh, she could get used to this, too. Her back arched, her inner muscles clenching him tight. That must've done it for Nick followed her climax and roared his release. He shuddered over and over. He caressed her legs as he slowly withdrew.

"Time for brunch."

Ronnie reached for her glasses by the bed. "You're incorrigible."

Nick laughed and stood. "You love it."

No, Nick, I love you. She paused for a moment, did she say that aloud? But Nick had already headed to the bathroom not breaking his stride, so apparently she didn't. The words were going to slip out sooner or later, then—she knew. She would be hurt. Again.

*

An hour later, they sat curled up on the couch watching *The Today Show*. The odor of bacon still hung deliciously in the air, intermingling with the smell of simmering coffee. The man could cook. The brunch he prepared had been satisfying to the extreme. Fluffy scrambled eggs with chives and shredded cheese, bacon, toast, hash browns, and she ate it all. She was ravenous. She even had a second helping of hash browns. Now as she lay in his strong embrace, she was ravenous for something else. She stroked his chest, feeling the ripple of muscles through his shirt. Her hand climbed higher caressing his soft goatee. How she loved the feel of his facial hair caressing her bare skin.

She leaned in, inhaling deeply. His essence, so appealing, whether it was the aftershave he used or just his own musky, spicy scent or a combination of both. Veronica laid a feather-light kiss on the corner of his lips. He at last tore his eyes from the TV and looked down at her.

"What's up, sweetheart?"

Oh, she loved that he called her that now. It rolled off his tongue like melted butter. Her hand dropped to his crotch. Nick was semi-erect. Slipping her hand under the waistband of his sweatpants, she gripped him and stroked. He grew larger in her hand, as hard as stone: like velvet over hardened steel. His head fell back against the sofa and he moaned.

"Oh, Jesus. When you touch me," he rasped huskily. "Do it, baby. Stroke my cock—make me come."

The words sent a wave of molten, liquid heat straight to her core. Nick lifted his hips for a second and lowered his sweatpants just enough to give her full access. She smiled. The temptation to kiss his shaft was hard to ignore. Lowering her head, Veronica flicked her tongue across the head. Nick shuddered, his head snapping back up, his eyes wide.

"Just a taste," she said.

She moved her hand up and down the length of him, finding a quick rhythm that had Nick groaning. His breath quickened, his chest rising and falling. He climaxed, he laid his large hand over hers as she pumped his release. The hot essence of him covered her palm. His breath regulated at last.

"Listen to me, Ronnie. What we've shared—all of it—I've never shared with another woman. It never felt this good. Never. Do you hear me?"

She nodded, moved by his words. She knew what it took for him to admit such a thing. With her hand still on his crotch, she kissed him on the lips.

Veronica moved to his ear and bit his earlobe, then whispered, "I've never shared this before with any man. Never. The sex. The intimacy. I want more."

Nick leaned his forehead down to touch hers. "So do I."

*

An hour later and Ronnie had left for home. His place felt empty, and he felt—bereft. He could feel her presence everywhere. He picked up the pillow she laid her head on all night and inhaled her essence. He glanced at the kilt lying on the back of the chair and smiled. How many times did she reach the heights of ecstasy? This was a night he'd never forget. He picked up a pearl button from her blouse. She must've torn three or four of them off in her haste to undress. He placed the button on the end table.

His gaze focused on the rumpled bed. How many times did they make love? He lost count. Four, five—he closed his eyes. The smell of her scent, the feel of her skin, those blue-gray eyes that looked at him with such intense desire and passion moved him. Did he read more there? Did he *want* to read more in her eyes? This had progressed far too fast and was becoming far too intense. He walked to the kilt and ran his long fingers over the rough wool. Why did he order this? To please her and make her happy. He loved it. Perhaps he *was* beginning to fall in love with her. Was it love? He didn't know what it felt like. Only had that damned puppy love with the schoolteacher to go by and that had been frigging agony. The songs all say it: love hurts, love bites, love stinks. He agreed, 110 percent—all the way.

This didn't stink and it didn't hurt—only when she was apart from him. Wasn't that love? Not wanting to be apart from the person? His feelings were so powerful they disturbed him. He wanted to sink into her softness and stay there, days at a time, revel in her curves, and suck those luscious breasts. He wanted her to share—everything—with him. He wanted cinnamon buns on a Sunday morning with her and only her.

Nick stripped the bed, but he left the pillowcase, the one she'd laid her head on. He would sleep tonight with it close. Christ, like the song said, "he had it bad and that ain't good."

Should he pull back and keep his distance like he did with every other damned woman? If he was smart, he would. The honest truth? He couldn't stay away. Ronnie was strong, loving, giving, and funny. Nick flopped across the partly torn apart bed.

Oh, shit. He *was* in love with her. How the fuck did that happen?

*

It was fifteen minutes before one in the morning, Nick's Monday night closing time. He locked the door behind the last two patrons who staggered down the street happily drunk and singing Guns N' Roses songs. Exhaustion rolled through him, Ronnie had worn him out and he ached all over. Maybe he'd swing by her bakery tomorrow morning early, drop by with coffee. Yeah, he wanted and needed to see her again, he could admit that much to himself. Lorcan came by an hour before closing and they'd talked. He was tempted to discuss Ronnie and what he felt, but he still found it hard to verbalize emotions. He wasn't used to confiding to a friend, hell, he wasn't used to having a friend. So he said nothing as he usually did. If he couldn't even talk about it with Lorcan, how in hell could he ever talk about it with Ronnie? He kicked a nearby chair in frustration.

Wrecking the joint wasn't the answer. He leaned down and set the chair upright. A cleaning crew came in three nights a week. It used to be seven, but with the economy in a downturn he had to make a few cuts. He and Kevin picked up the slack, tonight was his turn. Rubber gloves and Comet, coming up. He hated cleaning toilets and urinals. When men had a few beers in them their aim became lousy. Nick headed out back to the storage closet to collect the mop and bucket. He had a date with Mr. Clean.

*

Outside, Ronan McCarthy watched the bar as he had for the last couple of weeks. He knew the big biker bastard's routine now. Tonight he would stay late and clean before retiring upstairs to his flat. The time was now. Ronan tightly gripped the gas can handle in his gloved hand. The place looked ancient. He noticed when he came in the bar a few weeks back there was a sprinkler system, but he could do a lot of damage before they kicked in to any great assistance.

The place wouldn't burn to the ground, but he wanted to inflict enough damage to equal his revenge. This to his twisted mind was of paramount importance. *Striking the name out in my book.*

He glanced around, it was late and the street quiet. The bar was situated at the bottom of a hill and somewhat isolated. Empty warehouses surrounding it and the half moon illuminated off a few broken windows and worn bricks and mortar. A nearby elevated train whizzed past, sparks from the track fluttered down below giving a brief smattering of light.

Ronan doused the building with the gasoline. His nostrils flared in protest as the nauseous petrochemicals seeped through his nasal cavity. *Blimey, why some people sniffed this stuff.*

He worked quickly and efficiently. He was no firebug, had not really started a fire before on this scale, but he did do a lot of research. *Got to love the Internet.* A cruel smile curled about his thin lips. If the biker got a little toasted, then all the better.

*

Lorcan grumbled as he drove toward Nick's bar. How the shite did he leave his wallet on the table? *Eejit.* As he turned onto Prince William Street and headed down the hill, he gazed into the night sky. A strange orange glow hovered above Nick's bar. He hit the accelerator and the back end of his rented Lincoln Navigator banged on the pavement leaving sparks from the under carriage.

Nick's bar was on fire.

Lorcan's SUV squealed into the parking lot. Nick's bikes were in their usual spots. He jumped out of the Lincoln before he barely slammed it in park. Flames poured out of the building. Lorcan kicked at the huge oak door. *That bugger is not going to give.* He ran around back, the steel door was locked tight. Grabbing an empty wooden vodka crate, Lorcan sprinted back around front and sent the heavy crate careening through the window. The glass blew apart and flames roared out and then just as quickly were sucked back into the building. Lorcan climbed through the window, not caring his hands were getting cut on the jagged glass.

The sprinklers had come on, not the best with regards to the water pressure, but it did the job. The flames were being contained, but where was Nick? Kicking aside tables and trying not to slide in the water that quickly accumulated on the wood floor, Lorcan raced to the back rooms.

"Nick!" he yelled.

Did he hear a groan? Kicking the men's bathroom door open, he found Nick on the floor unconscious. Flames were making a meal out of his arm. Lorcan took off his jacket and smothered the fire, but he could smell the horrid, acrid smell of burning flesh. He reached in his pocket for his newly purchased iPhone. He almost dialed 999. *Get control Lorcan, you're in America, 911.* He called it in, and then shoved the mobile back in his jeans. He tried to move Nick, no luck. Christ, the bugger was heavy. Lorcan glanced outside the open bathroom door. The fire was nearly out, but Nick's bar appeared to be in tatters. He looked up at the ceiling; at least the flames didn't spread upstairs. Sirens wailed in the distance. Over and above the smell of burnt wood, leather and skin, Lorcan could smell one other odor. Gasoline. *Jaysus, someone set fire to the bar.*

Chapter Eighteen

Veronica paced the floor of the waiting room at Rockland General. Lorcan sat nearby, his gaze closely watching her nervous march across the tiles.

She wrung her hands to keep them from trembling. The doctors were examining Nick. When Lorcan called her, she thought she would break into pieces from worry. She can't lose Nick, she can't. The thought of it ripped at her heart. She loved him. Fiercely. Completely.

Of course, she said none of this to Lorcan. She glanced at him. He was a hero in her eyes. Since she met him on the double date, Veronica came away from that evening with a rather low opinion of him thanks to Julie's reaction. She'd misjudged him.

Nick didn't hand out friendship to just anybody. The only explanation is he must've sensed something in this man. What would have happened to Nick if Lorcan hadn't shown up? Smoke inhalation, more severe burns, maybe even death. It didn't bear thinking about.

"Come and sit, you're wearing a hole in the tile, darlin'," Lorcan soothed.

Veronica nodded and took a seat opposite him.

"Please, tell me the truth. You saw—how bad is it?" she whispered.

"It was dark and smoky, I couldn't see much. Let's wait and see what the doctor says."

Her eyebrows knotted in worry. "I've no idea how to contact his parents. He told me his mother's in Nebraska, his father's in New York City. He really has no contact with them, has he said anything to you?"

"No, darlin'. Nick certainly plays it close to the vest. You knew him from before when you were younger?"

"He moved here in the twelfth grade, I was in the tenth. He was almost as big as he is now and just as intimidating. When he walked down the hall people got out of his way. He was very quiet, brooding even. Then in March he dropped out," she laughed shakily. "I knew who he was and found out he knew of me, but we had never spoken."

Lorcan leaned back, his arms outstretched. "But here you are years later. Aye, it's fate. Destiny. You care for him, darlin'. I can see it."

She nodded quickly. Before she could reply, the doctor walked out of the examination room. Veronica shot to her feet. Lorcan stood next to her and laid a hand on her arm as if to steady her.

"Miss Barnes, Mr. Byrne? Nick Crocetti is resting now. We sedated him for the pain and he can't have visitors so perhaps you should head home. You can visit tomorrow afternoon. Nick has first-degree burns and a few second-degree ones. The burn on his arm is the most serious. We'll be watching that to ensure infection doesn't set in," Dr. Murphy turned to Lorcan. "Mr. Byrne, have you been checked out for smoke inhalation and had those cuts treated?"

"Lorcan! I never asked after you at all!" Veronica turned and looked up at him. "And I never thanked you properly. If you hadn't come back, I shudder to think what would've happened to Nick."

Lorcan patted her arm gently. Glancing over, he nodded at the doctor. "Aye, I did." He held up his bandaged hand.

The doctor left.

"I'm fine, Veronica. Don't fret. A little smoke won't hurt me." Lorcan seemed quite touched by her concern and her sincere thanks. "Come, I'll drop you off at home. Nick is resting. We'll come back tomorrow, I promise."

*

The next morning, Veronica busied herself in the bakery, taking inventory of the baked goods she'd prepared. Returning home from the hospital at three in the morning, she began to bake until the sun came up.

She overdid it with the cookies and didn't prepare enough rolls. Forget cinnamon buns, it reminded her too much of Nick. Perhaps she would make some later, especially for him. The hospital informed her Nick could have visitors after one in the afternoon. Julie would cover for her today.

Her mind raced all night while she found herself up to her elbows in dough and chocolate chips. Nick's place upstairs, would it be livable? Did he have insurance? What was he going to do, refurbish, renovate and re-open? That could take weeks and months. What would he do in the interim? Would he stay with her? Or maybe stay with Lorcan? Where did Lorcan live anyway?

No, she wanted Nick with her. Veronica wanted to care for him, hold him close in her arms every night and feel his warmth, his masculinity. She'd almost lost him. That she could not bear. She had her weekly phone call to her mother last night. She told her about Nick, that she had fallen in love with him. Telling her made the feelings real and potent. But this incident? It cemented her emotions permanently. Yes, she loved him and she did not want to lose him, ever.

The bell over the door rang and brought her thoughts back to the task at hand. Julie had arrived for her shift.

Julie stuffed her purse under the counter. "Any word on Nick?"

"Yes, he's awake and he's eating. He can have visitors this afternoon."

Julie patted her back. "Well, that all sounds good! You go, don't worry about a thing. I can hold the fort here no problem."

The bell over the door tinkled again, and Lorcan Byrne strode into the bakery. Julie immediately stiffened, her face drained of all color. After that double date at the pub as they both drowned their sorrows in white wine and peanut butter cookies, Julie confided she knew the reason she acted the way she did in Lorcan's presence. His handsome visage brought up so many damned, cruel memories, which made no sense as none of those hurtful and humiliating reminiscences were Lorcan Byrne's fault. Julie whispered that when he fixed her with that deep, penetrating gaze she felt he'd seen clear inside to the fat, lonely girl she used to be.

"I have to go out back, check on something," Julie mumbled.

Lorcan shook his head as she hurried out of the room.

"I must have the plague," he murmured.

Veronica didn't know what to say. If ever there were two people at cross purposes. She couldn't think about that now, her mind remained firmly fixed on Nick. She ducked out back to grab her purse. Julie leaned against the baking table. Veronica laid a hand on her shoulder.

"We're leaving now. You'll be okay to handle things?"

Julie's eyes glistened with unshed tears. "Yes, I'm okay."

Veronica didn't have the time to talk this out. She kissed Julie's cheek and hurried out front to go with Lorcan to the hospital.

Sitting in his Navigator, Veronica wasn't sure if she should bring up the subject of Julie. Best not, Julie would be upset if she told this man very much. After all, he really showed no interest in her, did he? She glanced at him as he weaved in and out of traffic. He wore dark sunglasses so she couldn't see his eyes.

"You seem used to our roads. Must be different for you, also the side the steering wheel is on."

Lorcan smiled. "Aye, but I do have to remind myself what side of the road to be on constantly. I'm managing."

"Are you staying, as in permanent? Do you have a green card, or do they give …"

Veronica shouldn't be asking these questions. None of this was her business. Since last night she found she wanted to get to know him. He was Nick's friend and she found she wanted him to be her friend, too.

"Are you asking if they give green cards for gangsters, is that what you mean, darlin'?" Lorcan said.

"Are you a gangster?" she asked.

Lorcan shrugged. "I work for one. I run his club. I earn a fair bit of nicker …" He turned and looked down at her over the top of his sunglasses, his aqua eyes twinkling. "That's money, darlin'. Guilt by association I guess it's called. Do I do more for him than that? Maybe, maybe not. I'm not lily white, but I'm not pitch black either. Does that make you tremble all over?"

Veronica crossed her arms. "I'm not some hot house flower. My brother's a cop. I've heard and seen plenty here in Rockland and living in California. I'm not afraid of very much. I'm not afraid of you."

Lorcan laughed. The lilting, musical chortle of a mordant Irishman.

"Good, darlin'. One thing you're afraid of is something happening to Nick. I saw the look on your face at the hospital. You care very much for him."

She couldn't deny it, he spoke the truth. She had fallen in love with Nick, as hard as she tried to fight it. It happened so fast. He charmed her socks off and other pieces of her clothing. He was stoic, commanding, and very masculine. The man was rugged to the extreme, but inside, vulnerable and lonely and maybe even damaged emotionally. How she wanted to be the one woman to breech the chasm in his heart, heal it, hold it for her own. Claim it—her and no other. She wanted to be the only woman to caress that skin, kiss those lips, and hold him close. Let him dive deep into her very core—him and no other. Veronica didn't want to share him with any women. He certainly made reference to his many affairs enough, yet he was not bragging, just making a statement of fact. For Nick was nothing if not honest, except about his deepest feelings and emotions. That was off limits. The protective fence remained in place for all the intimacies they'd shared. He allowed occasional glimpses through the slats. There was no two ways about it. She'd have to go first. Declare her love and damn the torpedoes.

She turned and gazed at Lorcan.

"I love him, Lorcan. Whether he wants to hear it or not, I'm going to tell him. Today."

For all her brave talk of not being afraid, she was shaking in her leather loafers over facing Nick. How terrible were his injuries? What would be his reaction to her declaration?

Ten minutes later, they arrived at the hospital and Lorcan stayed in the waiting room. She walked through the open door of Nick's semi-private room. A curtain had been pulled around the other bed. Low murmurs came from behind the barrier, so the person must have a visitor. Pushing her glasses up on her nose, she turned to gaze at Nick.

He sat up in bed wearing nothing but hospital sleep pants. The bandages wrapped around his chest and his left arm was clearly visible. A thick, mesh netting covered his arm as it rested on a couple of pillows. Veronica couldn't stop a gasp of shock from leaving her lips. Nick looked like a little boy. A tray sat in front of him consisting of half-eaten toast, a small plastic bowl with the prerequisite green Jell-O, and what appeared to be watery coffee. She blinked back tears and started to feel a little angry. She could care for Nick better than this. The food wasn't fit for a hobo.

"Hi, sweetheart," he croaked. His voice was hoarse from the smoke inhalation.

She sat on the side of the bed and cupped his cheek gently.

"Can you talk, is it too painful?"

"I can, hand me that water, though."

Veronica reached for the water and held the straw to his lips.

"I'll get you fresh bottle. First Nick, are you going to be all right? You have burns? How serious are they?"

"Chest—first degree, more like singed hair." He swallowed more water. "Arm, second degree. I didn't go into shock so I'm here for a few days until they rule out infection."

Veronica instinctively reached out toward the bandaged arm, but didn't touch.

"Will there be any scarring?"

The thoughts of his glorious, golden skin being marred in anyway cut her deeply. His discomfort and pain upset her. The burns had to hurt like hell.

"Very little. I was lucky Lorcan arrived when he did." He pushed the water away.

"Nick, you're coming to stay with me." She held up a hand when he started to protest. "We don't know what condition your apartment's in, and you need someone to assist you. I want to do it, Nick. I want to be there for you."

Veronica leaned closer and cupped his cheeks. "Listen to me. I love you, Nick. So very much. Let me care for you—let me love you."

She kissed him softly. Dropping her hands, she sat back and observed the confusion on his face. She had the feeling no one ever said the words to him before in his whole life. He didn't know how to react: it was painfully obvious. She laid a finger on his lips.

"Don't say anything, Nick. I know it's a lot to take in. We have a lot to talk about, but not now. You'll be coming home with me." She stood. "I'm going to go get you a bottle of fresh water and let Lorcan come in for a minute."

She left the room.

*

Nick looked off out the window. White, puffy clouds languidly rolled by. A few trees planted in the courtyard outside swayed gently in the breeze. A lone tear rolled down his cheek.

"Nick, mate."

Lorcan had arrived. Nick's head was still turned toward the window and he was so deep in thought he never heard his friend enter.

Nick turned to face him. He tried a brief, wane smile and motioned to the chair.

"Take a seat."

"You're looking better," Lorcan said.

"Thanks to you," Nick replied hoarsely. "I could've been a charcoal briquette if you hadn't come back. For your wallet, you said. Sorry—lost in the fire. How much, I'll pay you back."

"Feck that, mate," Lorcan dismissed.

"How did I get a semi-private room? I've no medical insurance. I should be in a ward."

"I took care of it. No worries. Speaking of insurance, did you have any on the bar?"

Nick nodded, clearing his throat. "Yes, enough to rebuild, how— how bad is it?"

Lorcan pursed his lips. "Mostly smoke and water damage. The fire didn't spread upstairs, though you may have smoke problems. The bar itself—sorry, mate. It's a write off I'm guessing. The fire inspectors will let you know if the building's still structurally sound. The fire was quickly snuffed out by the sprinklers so it might be all right. You own the building?"

Nick nodded again. "Received the building for next to nothing. The money I used as a down payment was for services rendered. You know what I'm saying?"

"Aye," Lorcan said. "I do at that."

"I financed the rest with a fencing operation I had going years back and a loan from a relative. I make a small profit in the bar enough to live on, not much else. I'm fucked, Lorcan. What am I going to do, bake cookies for Ronnie?" Nick started coughing.

Lorcan stood. "No more chin-wagging, mate. Look, you can work with me until you get this shite insurance muck straightened out. Hell, you can stay with me, too. I've lots of room."

Nick nodded again. "Thanks, about the job. I'll take it. Ronnie asked me to stay with her."

"Oh, aye? Interesting development."

Nick shrugged and glanced out the window again. His entire body was still numb, and it wasn't the damned painkillers. Her words kept playing over and over in his head. *I am in love with you*—what was he to do with that information? Did she even mean it? After the initial shock wore off, he began to wonder. Perhaps she felt sorry for him because of his injury, the fire, and his bar. Or was he feeling sorry for himself?

No one ever said those words before. Not his parents, not his teacher-lover, or the myriad of women that followed. No one. Ever. She wanted to talk, great. He hated talking about his feelings or anyone else's.

Ronnie had returned. She held a bottle of water. Lorcan whispered in her ear and left the room. Nick's throat was killing him. He talked far too much and this was a perfect excuse not to talk to her about anything she declared in a moment of weakness.

"Lorcan will wait outside. The nurse at the station said I can only stay for a few more minutes. Can I get you anything, magazines? Books? Crossword puzzles?"

He shook his head.

Ronnie opened the water bottle, stuck in a fresh straw, then sat on the edge of the bed and held it for him. He took a long drink. The water was cold and crisp. Ronnie leaned in close. He could smell the essence that was hers alone, intermixed with the enticing smell of cookie dough. He'd bet even money she stayed up all night baking.

"I meant what I said, Nick. In case you were lying here doubting my word. I love you. *Love.* You. Get used to it, because I'll be saying it a lot." She kissed his cheek tenderly. "Love, Nick. The forever type. The share everything type. The passion type. The 'I will look after you in sickness and health' type. You're coming home with me, agreed?"

What could he do but nod?

She stood and left the room.

He was alone.

Love. A foreign state to him. Yesterday morning when she had gone home he'd felt her absence. It left a gaping wound, aching and sore. He did want her to look after him, care for him, hell—love him. His emotions all started to fall into place. After only a few weeks? Hell, why not?

The feelings filled him with trepidation. He knew nothing about the giving and taking in a relationship, not really sure he was even capable. He thought of no one but himself since he was a kid, when it was obvious back then that no one else cared. He decided at that time he would look out for *numero uno:* see to his pleasures and needs. He could be a selfish being.

These last few weeks with her, had he acted selfish? He did things for Ronnie he never dreamed he would do for a woman. Dress up as a Highlander. Cook meals. Invite her to spend the night more than once. Tell her things—*Awww, hell.*

Glancing out the window again, he listened to birds chirping in the trees. Why did he cry? Okay, he didn't blubber, but a damned tear rolled down his cheek after she left the room the first time, after she said the words. He hadn't teared up since he was a kid. The desperation to hear the words, was he that damned grateful?

No, he had to stay resolute, firm, and guarded. He had to protect his heart. He couldn't lose control of his emotions. He fought so hard to keep them reined in all these years.

Nick closed his eyes, he needed sleep. God, he was so damned weary.

Chapter Nineteen

Driving back toward the bakery, Veronica remained silent during the entire drive. Lorcan glanced at her.

"Well darlin', don't keep me hanging. Did you tell him?"

"Yes, I did," she replied softly.

"I thought as much. Never seen a man so confused and flummoxed as Nick. You rocked him, Veronica. To his core, I'll be guessing."

"I suppose so. It's not going to be easy."

Lorcan laughed. "Ah, but that is the challenge when it comes to true love. I have a romantic soul. It will all work out, believe me."

"Have you ever been in love?"

"No, not really. Maybe someday. I can hope."

"I thought I was once, even had a quickie Vegas marriage. I was so wrong. It's nothing like I feel for Nick. Nothing."

"Nick is not an easy man, but stick with him, you won't be sorry," Lorcan soothed.

"Thank you, Lorcan, for everything."

He pulled into her small parking lot.

"Will you come in? I'll make tea or coffee, I have fresh baked goods."

Lorcan looked at the large front display window. Julie stood, watching them. As soon as their eyes met she walked away. Jaysus, why did he even care what this Julie thought of him? What in hell did he do or say for her to treat him with such scorn? Anyway, he had an errand to run, an important one.

"Cheers, darlin'. I'll take a rain check. I'll call you tomorrow."

Veronica climbed out of the Navigator and waved as she headed for the front door of the bakery.

Lorcan took one last look at the large window. He took his sunglasses from the visor and put them on. Julie stood off to one side still watching him, no doubt thinking he couldn't see her. Perhaps she was not as uninterested as she let on. She was not the type he usually went for. Yet, there was—something. Every time their paths crossed his gaze was drawn to her. He couldn't explain why and he spent a few sleepless nights trying to work it out. He shook his head and peeled out of the parking lot leaving a trail of rubber in his wake. He had bigger fish to fry.

Ten minutes later, he arrived across town at the rented rooms his cousin, Ronan McCarthy, resided. He knew he would still be there as he didn't go into the club until six o'clock. Lorcan took the stairs two at a time, then pounded on the door. Muffled music played inside so the bastard was in there. He pounded harder.

"Open up, Ronan, now!"

The door opened and Ronan snarled, "What the feck?"

Lorcan pushed past him. "Pack your bags, you gobshite."

"Not a bloody chance, cousin."

Lorcan strode to the dresser and pulled Ronan's clothes out and tossed them at him.

"Pack, now. You're going back to Dublin."

Ronan laughed. "Why? Old man De Luca not happy with me?"

Lorcan kept emptying the drawers, slamming them shut as he did.

"I'm not happy with you, mate. You set fire to that bar, The Chief. I know your black soul. Get out. I'm giving you the push."

"You've no proof, and you've no authority over me," Ronan's face twisted into a sneer.

Lorcan turned and took three giant strides toward his cousin. Lorcan was close to five inches taller so he glared down at him then grabbed him by the scruff of the throat and pushed him up against the wall.

"Aye, I do. All the authority I need. Go back home and I'll not tell De Luca what you did. You know how he feels about going off the reservation."

Ronan struggled under Lorcan's tight grip. "He won't believe you."

"Oh aye, he will. I'm his little pet. He'll believe me sure as shite." Lorcan gripped tighter. "Why, what was the reason, some cheap thrill? Decided to add arsonist to your long, sick list?"

Ronan smiled a cruel, smug grin. "He pissed me off, that biker scum. He deserved it. He was in my book. You're going to be there and all."

Lorcan's blood boiled. He only had his gut saying it was Ronan. Now, turned out his gut was right. What should he do, call the coppers? There was no real proof. Besides, this rested on him, never should have brought Ronan. Also, for good or ill, Ronan was family. Getting him the hell out of town seemed to be the only answer. He and his cousin were the same age, grew up together. They had been involved in criminal activities since they sprouted hair on their clackers. They really weren't close; no one ever managed to get close to Ronan. The man had no humanity. He pulled Ronan from the wall and threw him across the room.

"Pack, I'm taking you to the airport. You're leaving now and you are never to return. Any money owed, I'll send along when you send me proof you're back in Dublin: proof of an address with your name on it. I want Auntie Vera calling me saying you're sitting at her table eating biscuits and drinking tea, you follow?"

Ronan's eyes narrowed, his face showing pure hate.

"Aye, I follow."

*

Veronica walked into her bakery. The burning sensation in her eyes became worse, no doubt from lack of sleep. Julie smiled and pointed toward the back.

"Your brother, Tyler, just arrived. He's in your apartment."

Veronica smiled wearily, "Thanks Julie, for everything."

Julie shrugged and returned her smile. "What are friends for?"

Veronica tossed her purse on the chair. There sat Tyler, his long legs out straight and crossed at the ankles, his hands behind his head. Soft music played from the TV.

"You got satellite TV, cool." Tyler stood and held out his muscular arms. He hugged her close. "I heard about Crocetti's bar," he whispered, his hand soothing her hair. "How is he?"

Veronica wiped a few wayward tears from under her glasses.

"A few first-degree burns, a bad second-degree burn on his arm. Oh Tyler, it could've been much worse. If his friend Lorcan Byrne hadn't arrived when he did, who knows? I shudder to think."

"Byrne, when did he and Nick become buddies?" Tyler asked.

She stepped back and looked at her brother. "You know Lorcan Byrne?"

"He works for Vinnie De Luca," Tyler said sternly.

"He runs his club, nothing else."

"I'll go see Nick tomorrow."

Veronica cocked her head. "You know Nick? When, from school?"

"I stopped by his bar a week or two ago."

"Oh, Tyler, you didn't! Were you in cop mode? Oh no, you were!"

Tyler reached for her arm and pulled them to the sofa.

"Easy. It's all right. We had a civilized conversation. Everything's fine."

Veronica sank back on the sofa and buried her head in her hands, her glasses going askew.

"Nick didn't tell you I stopped by, interesting. All right, I asked about his intentions."

Veronica stood again. She glared down at him, her fists clenched. She straightened her glasses and huffed.

"I can't believe you did that. What do you think this is, the fifties?"

Tyler laughed. He reached for her arm again and pulled her back down.

"That's just what Nick said. You guys seem to have a lot in common, righteous indignation at least. He told me to mind my own business.

I'm sorry I went over there, but I don't want to see you hurt. I love you, sis." He pulled her into a rough, brother-type embrace. "You should get some sleep, Ronnie. You're exhausted. I can see it in your face and hear it in your voice."

She sniffled. "I am. Nick is coming to stay here with me so I can look after him."

Tyler pulled back. "So this is serious?"

Veronica removed her glasses and rubbed her eyes in fatigue. "On my side it is. I love him so much, Ty. I told him so. And before you say anything, it's nothing like William Titus, nothing. Not even close. I know what I'm feeling. I'm not confused or addled or on the rebound."

Tyler laughed. "Okay. Fair enough."

"I think I will go lie down, but Tyler, can you come back tomorrow? I want to move the TV in the bedroom. I need help with the wires and hook-ups and such. I want Nick to be able to relax and watch movies while he recovers."

Tyler shook his head. "Sure, I'll come back tomorrow. Wow, you and Nick Crocetti. Never would've believed it."

Yes, her and Nick. It felt so right. So … real.

Chapter Twenty

Three days later, Veronica pulled into the parking lot of The Chief. Boards covered the broken front windows. A huge closed sign hung above the oak door with reopening soon right underneath it. Nick received the report from the County Fire Marshall and thankfully his building was still structurally sound. Reinforcements would have to be put in place to come up to the current code, but on the whole he could move forward with the cleanup and renovations.

The next step was a matter of sorting out the insurance money, finding a contractor, and deciding what to do with the renovations. Nick mentioned he wanted the bar to look as close as it did before. *First things first.* Tomorrow he would be released from the hospital and coming home with her. Infection hadn't seeped into his burns, thank god.

Veronica fished Nick's keys out of her purse. She was here to fetch clothes for him and to check the condition of the upstairs living quarters. Nick was worried even though the Fire Marshall said the damage had been kept to a minimum. The fire had been contained downstairs.

She slipped the key into the steel door and her nostrils were slammed with the odor of stale smoke, burnt leather, and wood. She glanced up to the top of the stairs to Nick's apartment. The door was closed. Maybe this fetid smoke smell didn't make it upstairs.

Curiosity gripped her so she poked her head in the bar. What she observed broke her heart. Nick hadn't seen it yet, he'll be devastated. All the hard work he put into the bar, a lot of it by his own sweat and blood from what he'd told her. The old bar and matching pool table were ruined. Nick mentioned they were decades old, original to the bar from the turn of the last century. Also those wonderful old wood floors were totally destroyed.

The jukebox Nick carefully selected all the music for—toast. All the classic Indian Motorcycle prints and collectibles—unsalvageable. She felt tears burn in the back of her eyes. She would help him any way she could to get his bar back in tip-top shape and open for business as soon as possible.

She climbed the narrow stairs to his apartment. Slipping in the other key, she opened the door. The smell hit her—smoke. Damn. Her nose crinkled in protest. She moved room to room opening any windows she could to let fresh air in, at least as fresh an air as you could get in Rockland. The Fire Marshall was right, no damage. The smoke odor would take a few days of airing out. Perhaps a professional crew should come in and steam clean everything for good measure.

Veronica stepped into his bedroom. She glanced at the bed. Memories of the past Sunday night flooded her mind. Closing her eyes, a moan escaped her lips. She'd never forget the nights they had shared. Never.

Opening her eyes she moved to the bed, he'd changed the sheets. You could bounce a quarter off it. She cocked her head at the mismatched pillow cases. One of the cases belonged to the sheet set he had on the bed when she stayed over. She picked up the pillow and brought it to her nose. He hadn't changed it because he wanted her scent close by. She hugged the pillow tight to her chest. A few tears escaped her eyes and rolled down her flushed cheeks. He did care and more than he'd let on.

She laid the pillow back on the bed then opened the closet and removed the duffle bag on the top shelf. The bag was right where he said it would be. She laughed softly. The closet was immaculate much like the rest of his apartment. Everything organized and orderly and he even had his shirts hanging according to color.

Tossing the duffle bag on the bed, she walked to the dresser and opened the drawers. Veronica giggled. The man even folded his boxer briefs. She grabbed a few pairs and threw them on the bed. Opening another drawer she found t-shirts, dozens of them, almost all of them black. She shook her head and tossed a few on the bed. Another drawer, this one was full of sweaters, all types and blends. *Why, Nick—you're a bit of a clothes horse and a little anal about folding.* She smiled as she thought of her own dresser drawers. She stuffed her socks and underwear in a drawer until she could barely close it. Nick, no doubt, would be fussy over what laundry detergent to use and how many rinses each wash received. Wonder if he used dryer sheets? She lifted a sweater out of the drawer and brought it to her nose and inhaled. Pure, masculine Nick, he could bottle this and sell it. Women would go nuts; hell, they did already. If he used dryer sheets then it must be unscented ones. She couldn't picture Nick wanting mountain spring rain scent on his clothes. He didn't need it.

How long he would be staying with her, Veronica had no idea. Opening another drawer, there were all the jeans and the khakis. Her hand reached out and touched the black slacks. Wow, how these fit him. She tossed them on the bed along with a few pairs of jeans.

She quickly stuffed everything in the duffle bag. Socks. Where would they be? She walked back to the dresser and opened a smaller drawer. Her jaw dropped open then she laughed. Nick folded his socks. She loved him. Living with Nick should be an adventure if nothing else. Great sex, great brunches, but he seemed to be a touch anal about organization. She could live with it. A little improvement in the organization department would be welcome.

Veronica glanced around, where was his washer and dryer? He had to have one. She couldn't picture Nick going to a laundromat using public machines, not if he was this careful with his clothes.

Glancing out into the hall, she noticed along one wall were folding doors. Veronica opened them. Above the washer a wire shelf held unscented dryer sheets and unscented, dye-free liquid detergent for sensitive skin. She giggled again, but closed the doors. Nick trusted her enough to give her his keys to his private sanctuary as he called it. She wouldn't betray that trust by rummaging around his private space like a scavenger, at least no more than she'd done already.

She walked back into the bedroom. One thing she did notice, there wasn't one photo of anyone in any room, which made her sad. She had pictures in frames on the wall, in her living room, by her bed—Nick didn't have one. His childhood really did suck. Well, she would make sure she and Nick made their own memories, enough to fill frames for every room.

Striding into his small bathroom, Veronica turned on the overhead light. As she'd noticed before, everything was neat and well organized. Open her medicine chest and Band-Aids and cotton balls would spill out on your head. Not Nick's. She gathered toothpaste, toothbrush, deodorant, aftershave, and other essentials. She found a toiletry bag under the vanity and threw everything inside.

After snapping off the light, she placed the toiletry bag in the duffle, zippered it shut, and walked into the living room. Sitting down the bag, she inhaled deeply. The windows would have to stay open for three hours at least. She would return later and shut and lock them.

She glanced around the living space, could she live here with Nick? The apartment was bigger than her place, but she needed to be by her business for the early morning baking. Nick's was a good ten-minute drive away. It would be pretty cramped at her home for the both of them long term. There was no room for Nick and all his media bling and his mountain of clothes. She shook her head. She should not get ahead of herself. Nick hadn't even said he loved her, let alone wanted some tight, close, exclusive relationship. In fact, he said the opposite.

Things had changed; she said she loved him. That declaration probably would send him back into his rabbit hole. They did have a lot to talk about and figure out. The next few days should prove to be interesting. Her thoughts were interrupted by the door buzzer. She ran down the stairs and opened the back door. It was a FedEx truck.

"Veronica Barnes?" She nodded. "Sign here." She took the pen and signed her name on the digital pad and he handed her the box. "Have a good day."

She cocked her head. *Vintage Lingerie*, Oh, my—the outfit. That's right; she'd ordered it in her name to come to Nick's address. Well, this should make Nick's week. She tucked the box under her arm and headed upstairs. He'd be in for a surprise. Perhaps before she went home, she would purchase the high heel white shoes like the model wore at the website. Veronica glanced at the bookcase. Nick would like a few books, but she'd no idea what he wanted. Maybe he had one in his night table drawer. She pulled it open and lifted out a paperback.

Highland Warrior Lover. He bought a romance novel, a historical, Highlander romance novel. He did it for her because she liked them. Flipping through the book, she noticed he'd underlined some of the Scottish speak. No wonder he knew those medieval Gaelic cadences. She hugged the book to her heart. He loved her. No man would go to all this trouble for a simple seduction, would he? Maybe Nick would, seeing how organized he was. She glanced at the kilt still folded neatly over the chair. He had gone to a lot of trouble, the meal, the kilt, and the sexy Scottish burr.

His actions were not mercenary. He did it for her—to make her happy. Nick cared more than he let on, more than maybe he knew. The revelation warmed her soul. She would have to bring Nick along gently here, not force him to admit more than he was willing to or he could very easily retreat back behind his protective fence.

She took the kilt, the book, and the FedEx box, and walked out of his bedroom. Picking up the duffle bag, she closed the door and locked it.

*

Nick's bandaged arm rested in a sling, but at least he could move it. Lorcan and Ronnie had picked him up and they just pulled into the parking lot of Titus Bakery. He felt apprehensive, not really sure why. Okay, he knew why. Staying with Ronnie—living together—even if it was for a few days or a few weeks filled him with dread. Staying overnight was one thing, but days and weeks?

Lorcan kept trying to take his arm as they walked toward the bakery. "I'm not an invalid!" he snarled.

"Easy, mate. Just lending a helping hand. Staying in a hospital bed for days can make you shaky on your pins," Lorcan replied.

"Yeah, right. Sorry, man."

Lorcan strode ahead and held the door open. Nick noticed Ronnie hovering close, but she didn't take his arm. He felt bad for snapping, but he was irritable and cranky. Not only the burns paining and itching, but the thought of his bar destroyed. He'd been questioned by fire investigators and police and got damned cranky with them too, asking if they were accusing him of torching his own bar for the insurance money. Yeah, that was a smooth move.

Thankfully, they didn't take his cantankerous mood to heart and stated he wasn't a suspect. That was all he needed, the cops breathing down his neck. He had enough of that back in Jersey. In the next breath, they said chances were they would never know who set fire to his bar. May have been dumbass teenagers looking for a thrill: that was their best guess. They questioned Nick thoroughly asking if he had any enemies, he couldn't think of any. He left Jersey and *the life* years ago. If anyone wanted to settle a score they would've done it long before now.

He walked into the bakery. Damn, he forgot how good it smelled. Maybe waking every morning to the odor of fresh cinnamon buns baking wouldn't be a bad thing. His mood lightened slightly. Nick inclined his head toward Julie in greeting and continued out back with Ronnie following right behind him.

*

Lorcan stopped and stared at Julie. Their gaze met briefly and then she grabbed the clipboard, turned her back, and started counting rolls. His mouth quirked into a smile. *Not today, darlin'.*

He strode to the counter and laid his hands palms down and watched her for several minutes. "I think you've already counted those twice." More seriously he said, "Turn around and look at me, Julie."

He watched her. Julie sat still with her back straight. Finally, she laid down the clipboard and turned to face him, her face devoid of emotion.

"Yes?" she said. Her voice was as cool as a Popsicle.

"I think Nick and Veronica are going to make it, as in permanent, do you agree?"

She glanced briefly at the back rooms, and then met his gaze again. Her look had softened.

"Yes, I agree. I think they'll be a couple if they aren't already."

"We'll be seeing a lot of each other if that's the case. You're friends with Veronica, I'm friends with Nick. We should try and be civil, don't you think?"

Lorcan leaned over the counter. Her eyes really were quite lovely.

She bristled. "I've always been civil!"

"Well, I won't belabor the point. You've been cool and standoffish and maybe with good reason. I've tried to go over in my brain what I may have done or said that offended or upset you. I can be an unfeeling sod at times. But I could think of nothing. If I did, I'm sorry. Can we start again? Who knows, maybe we can even be friends." Her head lowered. He'd have none of that. He gently lifted her chin. "Am I such a brute then?"

She smiled tremulously. "No, Lorcan. You're not. In fact, you're a hero. Ronnie told me how you ran into the fire and pulled Nick out. I think you're wonderful."

The words warmed his heart. So much so he found it hard to reply as emotion choked off his voice for a moment. He tapped her chin affectionately, and then moved his hand away. Reaching in his back pocket for his wallet, he inclined his head toward the rolls.

"Give me a dozen of those white pan rolls, darlin'. They look just like the ones my Auntie Vera used to make. Fresh rolls with currant jam and a pot of tea, nothing like it."

Julie moved to the rack of rolls. Grabbing a large paper bag and the tongs, she bent over. Lorcan's hands stilled on retrieving his wallet. Sweet Jaysus, but her arse was luscious. He closed his eyes briefly as he imagined his hands roaming over her lovely curves, grabbing handfuls of that arse, pulling her in close to the hardened part of him. His cock jerked to life and strained against his zipper. He snapped his eyes back open and she stared at him with a slightly puzzled look on her face.

Thank Christ the counter stood high enough to hide his blatant hard-on. What in hell brought that on?

"That will be $4.59."

He handed her a five dollar bill. Their fingers brushed together and he felt that roar of heat move up his arm, just as it did at the pub. She handed him the change, making sure their skin didn't make contact again. Perhaps she'd felt it too.

"So, we're cool?"

She smiled. The first time he had seen her smile fully, and it lit up her face.

"Yes, Lorcan. Everything is fine, we're cool."

"Ah darlin', you should smile like that all the time. Lights up the world it does." He backed up holding the bag of rolls in front of his obvious erection. "Maybe since we're going to try and be friends, we can go out to dinner sometime. Keep it in mind. Say my goodbyes to Nick and Veronica."

He turned quickly and exited, hurrying across the parking lot to his Navigator. He tossed the rolls on the passenger seat, climbed in, and pulled the door shut. He grunted from the discomfort, his stiff prick throbbed. He was as hard as an oak shillelagh. *Sweet Mary, what in the feck?* A little flash of luscious arse and he was off to the bloody races. She wasn't even that pretty. But those eyes of hers, he could drown in them. His hands gripped the steering wheel, his knuckles almost white. He raised his head. Julie watched him through the window, a puzzled look on her face.

Aye, you're not the only one confused and all, darlin'.

He turned the ignition and backed out of the parking place. This was dangerous. Maybe he'd been without female company too long. Perhaps he should take up the invitation from a few of the dancers at the club. They certainly made their interest known. No, not a good idea, maybe he should go up to Baltimore and see to his needs there. He didn't like people knowing his private business. He took one last look at Julie and roared out of the parking lot onto Waterloo Street.

Chapter Twenty-One

Early evening and Veronica had closed the bakery. Julie had gone home two hours before. She mentioned her and Lorcan spoke and agreed to be civil, maybe even friends. She was glad of that. She wanted their friends to get along. Did she see a little ray of hope in Julie's eyes? Maybe. Perhaps all Lorcan Byrne wanted was friendship. Hope Julie wasn't wanting more than that or she'd get hurt.

Veronica shook her head and walked into the apartment. She could hear the sounds of a ballgame down the hall. She opened the bedroom door, and there lay Nick, sitting up in bed watching the Orioles and the Yankees.

He wore jeans with his magnificent chest on full display. There were still bandages on his torso. A few of the lesser burns were pink, the skin puckered. She sat down next to him on the bed. Her hand moved across the burns, they were warm to the touch.

"Are they itching?"

"Like a son of a bitch. But scratching is more painful, I'm trying to keep my mind off it."

She giggled. "Sorry, shouldn't have mentioned it."

"Wait until they start to peel, that should be attractive. Shedding my skin like a damned snake," he grumbled.

She kissed his cheek. "Shedding means they're healing. It's a good thing."

He pointed to his arm. The second-degree burn was still bandaged tight.

"This hurts like hell. I hate taking those pain-killers, but I need them. I can't imagine someone badly burned. Jesus, it must be terrible."

She kissed him again. "You were lucky the sprinkler system snuffed out the worst of the fire, and lucky Lorcan came back when he did. Nick, if I'd lost you. I think that's when I realized how very much I loved you. The thought of you being taken from me—I couldn't bear it."

Veronica took his hand and their fingers laced together.

"Nick, the first time you came into the bakery you said you knew me from high school, or knew *of* me. How?"

"You caught my attention from the first. Sure, your looks and body sent my teenage hormones off the charts, but it was more than that. I watched you with your brother and your friends. You were everything I wasn't. Happy, content, confident—enjoying life. I admired you. Also, you were so brave. I was there when you stepped into that circle of girls and stood up for the fat girl they were teasing."

"That girl was Julie."

Nick's eyebrow arched. "Really? I had no idea. I was ready to step in myself. I've seen cat fights and they're vicious. No one was going to lay a hand on you while I was around."

Veronica's heart clenched tight in her chest. Her protector. Her love.

"Why didn't you approach me? Talk to me?"

Nick shook his head. "I wasn't fit company. I was angry a lot of the time. I would have made a lousy boyfriend. Besides, the princess does not date the school misfit. It isn't done." He squeezed her hand. "Hell, I am probably not fit boyfriend material now. How in hell did you know of me?"

"Nick, every girl in school knew who you were. You had the bad-ass aura around you. The fact you were near six feet tall and wore black leather and rode a motorcycle just added to the appeal. We all took bets, who would gather the courage to walk up to you and talk to you? I took that bet, and chickened out like the rest of them. You were every girl's fantasy. I watched you, too."

Nick sighed. "I never had sex with any girls from school. It was all talk."

Veronica smiled. "But the rumor about the schoolteacher was true."

Nick winced. "Yeah. Well, as I told you before, she offered something I needed and wanted. We were adults …"

Veronica placed two fingers on his lips to quiet him.

"She used you. She hurt you. She should have been reported. That woman crossed a line of trust. And as for you not being boyfriend material? Not true. You are giving, romantic, and sexy with just enough dark, dangerous masculinity to spice things up. Also, you are an incredible lover. Handsome, insatiable, and oh, so talented. You make great brunches, love old movies, and make fantastic potato skins. My god, no wonder I love you so damned much."

"Ronnie." His voice was rough, husky with emotion. "You might want to rethink that. There are things I haven't told you. About my past, things I did."

She let go of his hand, swung her legs over on the bed and sat upright next to him.

"You mean New Jersey, the Lucci Family?"

"How in hell …" His lips curled. "Of course, your cop brother. I should've known. He tried to warn you off me."

"He thought I should know everything. I knew you would tell me when you were ready. I know you don't like talking about your past. The good thing is—it's in your past, Nick. Did you ever kill someone?"

"What? No!"

"I didn't think so. So the rest of it's best forgotten. It's not your life now, is it?" she whispered.

Nick shook his head. "No. It isn't. I fenced goods, was a driver for one of the sons, did a little collecting, broke a few bones, that was the extent of my time with the Lucci's. I was a pebble of sand on that beach. I used the money I earned to make a big down payment on the bar. I borrowed the rest from Uncle Henry. I think he felt bad he'd left me in jail all that time. What did he know about being a parent or guardian? I think the money assuaged his guilt. I may be proud, but I took the offer. He never charged me interest and let me pay it back on my own schedule." He shifted uncomfortably on the bed. "Ronnie,

Lorcan offered me a job at his club bartending until my bar's back on its feet."

Veronica was floored. She couldn't get angry here or start nagging, she didn't want that kind of relationship with Nick, and she knew he wouldn't stand for it. It would remind him too much of his past.

In a calm voice, she said, "The De Luca's, Nick? Isn't that the Lucci's all over again?"

He shook his head vehemently. "No, Lorcan says the club is legit, I believe him. It would only be for a few months. I could use the money."

"You've only known this guy for a few weeks."

"Lorcan saved my life. That means something to me. I trust him."

He spoke with such emotion. He really cared for Lorcan, felt obligated and grateful. What could she say? Nothing.

"It's your decision. I'll back you on whatever you decide."

His eyes widened in surprise. He no doubt thought she'd rail and scream at him, that they'd argue and fight. That was not going to be their relationship if she could help it. She patted his leg and stood.

"Watch the rest of the game; I'll be back in a bit."

*

Nick watched her leave the room. Damn, she was glorious. His mouth quirked. Where was she going, out back where she kept the ball and chain?

She'd been his rock through this whole thing. Never thought anyone would be such a support to him like she'd been, and Lorcan too for that matter. He tried so hard to keep people at a distance. Thought he was above any emotion or need. Turns out, he wasn't. The surprising thing? He found he didn't consider himself weak for wanting that contact or that connection. His eyes drifted back to the TV, the Yankees just hit another home run. He picked up the remote and channel surfed.

Nick clicked back to the game, then to the Discovery Channel watching a show on sharks, then back to the game. He felt bored. Restless. He thought about their conversation. So they had both noticed each other in high school, felt a pull but did not act on it. As he said, it was for the best. It was funny how life turned out. More than ten years later here they were.

The door opened. Ronnie stood in the doorway, her hand behind her head in a classic pin-up pose.

His cock hardened immediately and with such a force he thought it would burst through his zipper. She wore the lingerie outfit they'd ordered over the Internet. He'd all but forgotten about it in the upheaval. He moaned aloud. The sound burst past his lips, he couldn't have stopped it if he tried. She looked stunning and he'd been right, she had the curves to pull it off. His heated gaze started at her high-heeled white shoes, her luscious legs encased in the sexy white stockings, up to the white, lacy corselet. She wore sheer white gloves past her elbows. Jesus, she even wore the pearls. Ronnie's hair was piled up on her head with soft tendrils framing her gorgeous face. Ruby red lipstick. She was a vision. Venus rising, like that damned painting by Botticelli. His goddess. Forever. She did this for him.

He stood. His legs shook from the intensity of his passion. Nick walked slowly toward her then dropped to his knees in front of her. He wanted to worship his goddess. He tossed off the sling; he didn't need it. Pain? Itching? He wasn't feeling a thing except desire—and more.

He reached out and embraced her legs, resting his face next to her midriff. His eyes closed, the feel of the silk stockings churned all manner of emotions in him. He lowered his head and kissed her leg, caressing and worshiping it. He moaned. He hung on for dear life. His hands moved higher over the corselet.

"Your body drives me wild. I love it," he rasped.

He stood and pulled her tight against him and ravished her mouth. His tongue plunged deep, taking total possession.

"Mine," he growled. "All mine."

She threw her arms around his neck.

"And you're mine, Nick. I'll not share you with anyone, ever."

He moved his lips down her neck, nibbling, licking and tasting.

"Ever. Never. No sharing. With no one."

He scooped her up in his arms.

"Nick, your arm!" she squealed.

He carried her to the bed and laid her down. "Don't feel a thing."

She was his, forever. He wanted no one else, no other woman but her.

He reached for the zipper on his jeans and in one smooth move was out of them and briefs. His cock stood at full attention.

He crawled on the bed and stood on his knees. His hands explored her again: The feel of her. The touch of her skin. Her scent. He slowly parted her legs. Ah, as he hoped the corselet held no barrier to the paradise that beckoned.

Nick didn't hesitate. Ronnie was wet; he could see it. His cock plunged in, neither mentioned a condom. This alone spoke volumes to Nick.

His goddess. He took her legs and wrapped them around his hips, then thrust even deeper. Hell, it felt so good. Gazing at her face, he observed she was close to coming. He pumped faster. She liked it this way, so did he. He slammed away. Her groans matched his. She cried out, bucking off the bed her peak so intense. Nick reached under her rear end and brought her closer. Sweat dripped off his forehead, he didn't care. He kept pumping. Ronnie's inner muscles contracted around his cock urging him on. She matched his powerful thrusts.

"Do it, Nick. Come inside me," she said seductively.

He poured himself into her, everything he was and hoped to be, all his loneliness and vulnerability and self-doubt. His very heart and soul, he poured it all, let it flow. Intense, soul crashing. His climax went on and on. He groaned with each shudder. She took it all, took all he had until he was utterly spent.

He withdrew, lay on the bed, and pulled Ronnie close to him. Never had he experienced that before. Never.

They both drifted off to sleep. Sometime later, he woke. Ronnie stroked his hair, murmuring to him softly. She kissed his cheek and stood, yawning and stretching.

"Ronnie."

"Yes, Nick?" she whispered, sleep heavy in her voice.

"I am in love with you."

She didn't reply right away, and then he heard a sob escape her lips.

"I love you too, Nick. So very much."

Ball and chain snapped around his ankle, he heard the metallic click. And he didn't care.

About the Author

Karyn lives in a small town in the western corner of Ontario, Canada. She wiles away her spare time writing and reading romance while drinking copious amounts of Earl Grey tea. Tortured heroes are a favorite. A multipublished author with a few bestsellers under her belt, Karyn loves to write in different genres and time periods.

As long as she can avoid being hit by a runaway moose in her wilderness paradise, she assumes everything is golden.

Karyn's been happily married for a long time to her own hero. His encouragement keeps her moving forward.

You can visit Karyn at *www.karyngerrard.com*.

A Sneak Peek from Crimson Romance
From *Prelude to a Seduction* by Lotchie Burton.

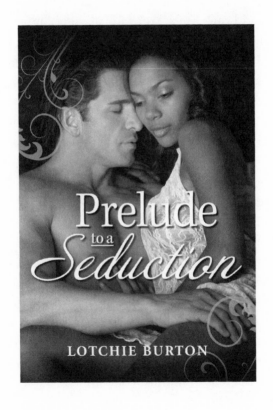

Prologue

"What are you doing?"

"I'm undressing you," he murmurs as his fingers deftly unfasten the buttons of her blouse and unzip her skirt. His mouth teases and nibbles at her neck and shoulder.

"Silly man, of course you're undressing me." She giggles. "Maybe my question should have been *why*?"

"Because," he whispers in her ear and lets his lips journey down her cheek to trail kisses across her chin and lips. "I love to touch your skin, and I can't touch you with all these clothes on."

Her smile is warm and sexy; her breath is hot and sweet. "I know, but if you keep this up, I'll never get out of here on time."

"That's the plan," he says, showing off perfect, beautiful white teeth in a wide, wolfish grin.

"I can't be late, not again!" She shrieks with laughter when he leans forward and licks that elusive sensitive spot just behind her ear.

"I'll bet no one will even notice. Come on, babe, let me send you off with a smile on your face," he cajoles. "Or at least let me send you off with a smile on *my* face." He grins and wiggles his eyebrows up and down. She shakes her head. He knows she'll eventually give up and give in to his persuasive mouth and convincing hands. Ignoring her feeble attempts at protest, he continues to methodically strip her clothing away piece by piece until she stands completely naked and exposed to his appraising gaze. He lays her down upon the bed and blankets her with his body, burying his face between her soft, succulent breasts.

"Mmm," he sighs in muffled contentment. "You feel so soft. I could lie here forever."

"We don't have forever," she purrs seductively, "and I can't wait that long. You've got me naked; you need to do something about it right now."

"I'm more than happy to oblige, my lady," he responds, his voice low and husky with need. "Your demand is my wish." He brushes and strokes her body with nimble fingers and knowledge-able hands, familiar with every curve, every dip, and every hollow. He knows her body in intimate detail, and he knows what it takes to make her hum, purr, and sing for him.

"I love the way you smell. You smell like ice cream," he murmurs and slowly kisses and licks his way down the length of her body.

"Ice cream?"

"Yeah, ice cream. I want to see if you taste like ice cream, too." He reaches his destination and settles himself between her legs, at the juncture where her silky smooth thighs spread and separate, and allow him access to her liquid heat. He pushes his face down into her heated crevice, inhaling deeply and drawing in the distinctly musky, sweet scent of her sex. His tongue flicks and licks and laps and tastes the gathering pool of nectar, generated by his skillful touch.

"You taste like caramel, like caramel over ice cream," he whispers against her sensitive bud. "Mmm, you're so sweet. I can never get enough of your taste." He continues to stroke her silken walls with his tongue and to tease her hidden pearl; then he dips deep inside to taste more. She moans and writhes from the pleasure.

"Oh, babe, it feels so good, but I want to feel you inside me. I need to have your hard, throbbing cock here." She uses her hand to point the way. "Inside me now."

He shudders with desire and rises to fulfill her urgent plea. He pushes her legs higher, spreads them wider, moving into position to plunge deep. Her moans excite him and stir and push him toward the edge. He presses the tip of his shaft at her entrance, anxious and impatient to feel her hot, velvet sheath wrapped and squeezing tightly around his—

BEEP! BEEP! BEEP!

David's eyes flew open to the recognizable sound of the alarm clock incessantly beeping, the noise loud enough to wake the dead. He came fully awake, his body taut, rigid, and aching with a raging hard-on, his cock hard enough to punch through steel. Damn! It was another damn dream! He groaned and angrily slapped the off button on his clock. Closing his eyes and resting his head against the headboard, he tried to breathe through his painful erection, knowing the feeling would subside as the memory of the dream faded. Unable to completely quell the desire that constantly rode him, he punched the pillow in utter frustration: hard, hot, and achingly unfulfilled.

Chapter 1

Sunday

Sarona Maxwell waited patiently for her turn at the hotel registration desk. She'd just arrived at the end of a long day...tired, hungry, and ready for a meal and a hot shower. This was the final leg of a three-week business trip. The current endeavor was a five-day seminar of classroom instruction and vendors' exhibits showcasing software and peddling technology. Though her hectic travel schedule was nearly over, she dreaded yet another week of crowded venues, too-small hotel rooms, and too much drama that came with the close proximity of too many people and personalities. When one was employed by corporate America, drama was an everyday occurrence. She was accustomed to events like this, and since these meetings occurred often it was likely she'd see associates she'd met before in some other city, at some other meeting. Maybe, she chuckled to herself, just once she'd be spared the usual host of pompous, superficial characters who were permanent fixtures in the world of corporate soap operas.

As she waited, she looked over her surroundings and admired the remarkable architecture and décor the hotel offered, impressive by anyone's standards. The lobby was huge and sported a glass wall front at the entrance, the height of which spanned the first two floors. The high ceiling was supported by giant square pillars, trimmed in rich walnut with mirrors on all four sides that picked up and reflected activity in every direction. Enormous crystal chandeliers, marbled floors, plush carpeting, and staircases in wood and brass worked in concert to impress and convey opulent elegance. Large sculptures, paintings, and works of art purposefully placed throughout the great expanse created a museum-like quality. The rich brown, green, and burgundy hues implied a sense of simple sophistication.

"May I help you, ma'am?" The cheerful voice of the hotel clerk brought her attention back to the front desk

"Yes, thank you," Sarona replied and presented her identification for registration. While going through the normal check-in and verification process, the clerk began to frown and mutter unintelligible comments.

"Is there a problem?"

"No, ma'am, I don't believe so, but there's been a change in your reservation that I need to confirm."

"What kind of change?" she responded, exasperated and concerned there might be yet another complication to add to an exhausting day already filled with changes and complications.

"Oh, no, ma'am, it's nothing serious. It seems you've been upgraded because we're overbooked. You'll still receive the quoted rate, but a much better room for the price," the clerk said with a bright smile. After the day Sarona had had, she liked the sound of "much better." She completed and signed the necessary paperwork, and the clerk thanked her for her patience and wished her a pleasant stay. Sarona gathered her things and left in search of the elevator, tiredly dragging her luggage behind.

Once inside her room, Sarona suddenly realized how understated and inadequate the terms "upgraded" and "much better" were to describe the change in her accommodations. The room was a suite, a jaw-droppingly huge suite. The décor was significantly different from that of the hotel lobby. There were various shades of bright corals, pinks, blues, and greens, with plush pillows of all sizes scattered over a sofa and two chairs. The carpet, a beautiful, sandy beige color, was luxurious, soft, and thick. The seating area was accented with brass and glass coffee and end tables, each sporting elegant crystal lamps, all arranged facing a 42-inch, flat-screen television mounted on the opposite wall. There was a small kitchenette and wet bar, complete with bar stools in highly polished brown maple and fabric that matched the sofa and chairs. The entire room overlooked a breath-taking view seen through sliding glass doors that opened onto a small balcony. Small, tropical trees and potted plants were placed all about.

Sarona dropped her bags and hurried excitedly to see the rest of the suite. Inside the bedroom, an enormous king sized bed occupied the center of the room, big enough to fit at least three people comfortably. The same colorful décor of the main suite was repeated here. Off to one side, a small alcove contained a seating area consisting of a loveseat, table, and chair placed in front of a large window.

In a state of shock, she made her way to the bathroom. The tub, slightly elevated, was unbelievably large and deep, with several jet sprays positioned all around. There was a separate shower stall with showerheads on three walls and one overhead. Situated next to it was a toilet and bidet enclosed in their own room. In the middle of the room was a long, low, wooden bench. The image of lavish excess was completed by shining brass fixtures and mirrored walls that reached all the way to the ceiling at each end of the tub.

"Oh, my God," she whispered. Stunned and nearly speechless, she leaned against the wall. "Oh, my God."

Still trying to shake off the shock of her discovery, Sarona gathered up her suitcases and began to unpack. As a rule she usually packed light, but with so many destinations in so many weeks, she had extra luggage. Among her usual travel necessities there were three things she considered essential and never left home without: earplugs for unexpected noises that could ruin a good night's sleep, socks for her constantly cold feet, and her vibrator for . . . uh . . .

tension release. She chuckled at the memory of a long-ago comment to her friend Joyce during one of their "woman-to-woman" conversations: "Girl, my vibrator is like American Express. I don't leave home without it." Her decidedly kinky twist on the well-known commercial had left them both bubbling with laughter.

Joyce Jeffers was Sarona's closest friend. They'd met four years ago during one of life's quirky coincidences—at an airport while waiting for a delayed flight. The two struck up a conversation over a mutual weakness for designer shoes and handbags and soon discovered they had more in common than the overdue flight home. During that two-hour wait, they developed an instant bond, which had blossomed into a relationship that had grown and strengthened over time. Joyce was a few years older and wiser and, as was expected with close friends, felt it was her duty to pass on her personal and professional experience and opinion, whether it was asked for or not. She fulfilled the prerequisite role of best friend and confidante and listened, encouraged, persuaded, or championed whenever called upon.

Sarona was an only child and had grown up isolated and alone, separated from the rest of the world by strict and overprotective parents. As a consequence of living a sheltered life, she was strong-willed, independent, and had a mind of her own. The down side was she often found it challenging to integrate herself into social situations. It wasn't that she disliked being around people—she disliked being around a *lot* of people, and unfortunately, her preference for privacy and solitude threatened to turn her into a recluse. She'd also discovered through experience that at times she could be a bit naïve when it came to understanding people and their motivations—another flaw she recognized and struggled to overcome. She fought to keep a balance between her gullible and accepting side and the other skeptical and suspicious side. For her, it was a fine line to walk, and having Joyce as a friend and mentor helped make sense of the differences between the two.

Sarona finished putting her things away, and giving her suite another appreciative survey, stared longingly at the bed. Although she could easily have fallen face down into the enormous bed and not come up for air until the next day, she was unable to ignore the persistent hunger signals her stomach kept sending to her brain. So, before she gave into the exhaustion that threatened to claim her, she decided a quick visit to the hotel restaurant would solve at least one of her problems.

An hour later, with her hunger sated, she ended her long day with a glass of wine and a blissful soak in that absurdly large tub. And then, finally, sank into the welcoming softness of a king-sized bed, fit for a queen.

*

Monday

The seminar kicked off with its usual fanfare: preliminary introductions of directors, board members, and chair members, all taking turns giving their own personal welcoming speech. There was, of course, the extended invitation to meet fellow forum members in a more casual environment during the obligatory first evening mixer. A promise of free hors d'oeuvres, beverages, and cocktails was sure to guarantee maximum participation.

At the end of the day Sarona returned to her suite. Putting away her training materials, she was torn between returning for the mixer or staying in and ordering room service. As usual, she would have preferred to spend the evening alone reading, but if she didn't show up she'd spend the next day as the subject of good-natured teasing and being accused of anti-social behavior.

It wouldn't be far from the truth—she had very little interest in socializing and found it difficult to change a lifelong practice of avoiding the ritual. It was easier to avoid the circumstances altogether than to make token appearances. Giving a sigh of resignation and chalking it up to one of those necessary evils, she changed out of her business attire into something more casual, and left to join the group . . . just for a while.

*

David stood back and away from the crowd, secluded and cleverly hidden from view. A large sculpture and the branches of a strategically placed potted tree shielded his position. He resembled an animal stalking prey, his eyes constantly in motion, scanning and searching the room until he found what he was looking for.

"Sarona, there you are," he murmured. He watched as she mingled and moved about the room, stopping every few steps to engage in small talk with the others. He'd become quite adept at reading her, and he watched now as she slowly and steadily worked her way across the large room, edging toward the nearest exit to undoubtedly make her escape. He tracked her movements toward her intended route, hazarding a guess at how long it would take her to disappear altogether. That was her M.O.—make an appearance to show her face, socialize for a short period of time, and then move on before anyone noticed. But sometimes, if waylaid by a particularly persistent individual, her retreat could be delayed for hours, and that was what he was counting on.

He'd picked up on this habit and other interesting details after a number of months spent observing how she moved and interacted. He knew her, and he knew she was biding her time and planning her getaway. Well, he had news for her—tonight it wasn't going to be that simple. She was going to have to stick around a bit longer, if he had any say about it. Tonight, he had a vested interest.

Though they'd only met a few times in the past, he found himself totally intrigued and captivated with her personality; the fact she was beautiful was simply an added bonus. His curiosity had been piqued by her lack of interest in the usual superficial trappings or the need to impress. With his considerable experience in pursuing women, it was something he'd rarely seen, and he wanted to learn more. However, his attempts to get to know her better were met with complications at every turn. He was acutely aware that she put up a wall between them whenever he tried to initiate conversation.

Oh, she was nice enough, polite, even friendly, but he could detect that in some way she was put off by him, and avoided him every chance she got. He didn't think she liked him very much, and he didn't have a clue why, so he took a perverse pleasure in hunting her down and forcing her to tolerate his company. Even though his actions were precipitated by his adolescent-like behavior, he'd discovered that he enjoyed being with her whenever he got an opportunity. He found her smart and witty with an outrageously wicked and teasing sense of humor . . . whenever she slipped and let her guard down. Then he was allowed a glimpse at something deeper and beyond her distant polite exterior.

It was their last encounter and conversation, repeated over and over in his head, that had put him on edge and had unexpectedly triggered an obsessive need to get closer. Something she'd said had haunted him and pushed his mind and imagination beyond their limit for far too many days and nights since.

David had waited six months for this moment. He wasn't even supposed to be there, but he'd wangled an exchange of venue with a co-worker. He knew Sarona would be there because he'd made the necessary checks and inquiries to make certain of it. This five-day conference was going to be his ticket to getting closer to her and getting to know her—intimately. He was limited in what he could do in only five days. The short amount of time would be a stretch even for his ability to charm and persuade, but he was optimistic. He had confidence on his side. He'd worked his magic and gotten what he wanted in far less time, so this situation should be no different. He'd spent the last six months immersed in total fantasy. He had tortured his poor mind and body beyond endurance with vivid dreams and visions of her beautiful face contorted in sexual ecstasy, her imaginary soft moans of pleasure echoing in his head. He'd made up his mind six months ago. There would be no escape for her this time. She would not be allowed to ignore him or brush him aside as she had done repeatedly in the past. This time she was going to have to deal with him face-to-face, one on one. He had plans for her, plans he'd already taken the necessary steps to put into motion. Somewhere along the way she had become his obsession, and he was going to have her, seduce her into bed, his or hers—it didn't matter.

David knew he had a certain, perhaps unsavory, reputation and that it preceded him wherever he went. Tales told and spread among the women he had been intimate with over time had seen to that. He'd learned at an early age there was something about him, something to do with his biological chemical makeup along with his striking good looks that attracted the opposite sex in droves. As a young boy, he had thought it was a curse and hated the uncomfortable situations he had suffered through with little girls practically chasing him everywhere he went. But, by the time he'd hit puberty, he'd discovered the true advantage he had in the hand he'd been dealt, and well . . . the rest was history. Women were drawn to him like moths to a flame, vying for his attention and affection, and he willingly obliged, for he was, after all, merely a man.

He admitted he liked the attention, but over the last year or so he'd grown tired of the role. Everything was too easy. There was no challenge and no excitement, and the outcome was always the same, at least until he'd met Sarona Maxwell. Sarona was elusive, unobtainable, her manner remote, mysterious, and she seemed always just out of reach. Her elusive ways intrigued and challenged him, and were all the more reason why he had to have her. He believed Sarona was just what he needed to revive his interest in the pursuit of a beautiful woman, because *this* woman certainly didn't make anything easy. Her avoidance of him approached to the point of snobbery, and he refused to be snubbed.

He continued to watch her undetected, studying her from his concealed position.

No, she wasn't the type he was normally attracted to, but to tell the truth, he'd become pretty damned bored with the type he was normally attracted to. Sarona was black—or was that African American? He was never sure which term was politically correct. He guessed she was probably in her early to mid-thirties, but not much younger than his thirty-six years. She was above average height—tall for a woman and only a few inches shorter than his height of six feet three inches. She had a full figure with large breasts and luscious curves, perfectly proportioned in an hourglass shape reminiscent of those old Marilyn Monroe films his dad used to watch on late night TV. Her skin was the color of caramel, the kind you see drizzled over vanilla ice cream, and it looked just as rich, just as creamy. Her hair was a rich, dark brown with streaks of mahogany and fell in long, wild and thick in layers down her back to just below her shoulders. She had a warm, beautiful smile and intelligent, dark brown eyes, deep enough for a man to swim in . . . or drown trying. He was drawn to, aroused by, and turned on by her dark skin, dark eyes, and dark hair.

He shuddered and hardened at an unexpected visual: the two of them with their limbs intertwined against a backdrop of soft candlelight, champagne, and satin sheets. His lips locked against the softness of hers, his tongue delving deep, seeking to taste the sweetness of her mouth. His hand cupped the fullness of her breast, stroking her dark nipple with his thumb, pressing his hard arousal firmly against her, maneuvering and thrusting to get deep inside her waiting, wet . . .

"There you are!" The familiar sound of Shelia Preston's voice startled him and brought him reluctantly out of his fantasy. "Everyone's been looking all over for you and lucky me, I'm the one who's found you." She all but purred her satisfaction.

Of all people, David thought with bitter resentment he miraculously managed to keep from registering on his face. Shelia was a former lover who refused to be relegated to the classification of "former." She constantly sought him out with the intent to lure him back, but there wasn't a chance in hell of that ever happening. That time was long past. He conceded she was a beautiful woman; that's what had attracted him. She was ultra-feminine, blonde-haired and green-eyed with a willow-thin body envied by the world's average woman, topped with today's must-have accessory, thirty-four DD silicone breasts. Although she was great to look at and an ornamental showpiece for any man's arm, her personality was about as interesting as sitting around and watching paint dry. Thinking back, he wondered what in the world he could have seen in her in the first place. Of course, thinking back, he had to admit personality hadn't been his primary consideration. He probably hadn't bothered to raise his eyes above her neckline.

"Hey, anybody home in there?" Shelia yelled as she shook his arm, once again bringing him back to the here and now. "Come on." She dragged him forward. "I want to show everybody I found you." Looping her arm into the crook of his, she led him out into the crowded room, preening and strutting like she'd just won a blue ribbon for the prize bull at the County Fair—a role David suddenly realized he was becoming all too familiar with, and one that left him feeling more like a prize than a person.

*

Sarona stood off to the side of the large room watching the crowd mill about, the mass of people conversing and networking with one another. She'd already met a few individuals she was marginally acquainted with earlier in the day, but so far she hadn't seen even one of them here. That made her wonder why she'd bothered making an appearance.

As she sipped wine and surveyed the room and considered whether she should call it a night, her gaze suddenly fell upon a familiar figure on the far side of the room. She knew who he was instantly, even though all she could see was his backside. She'd recognize that backside anywhere.

"Damn," she muttered. The "he" who caught her attention was none other than David Broussard. David was an extremely attractive man who stood about six-foot-three with piercing whisky brown eyes that shimmered like a mixture of bourbon and honey, rimmed by sinfully long dark lashes that had no business being on a man. His hair was a cap of coffee-brown curls, full and springy yet perfectly styled, trimmed and tapered to the nape of his neck. His facial features were strong and squared with lush, full lips and a straight, patrician nose, giving an impression of chiseled perfection equal to that of the Greek god Adonis himself. Flawless, golden-bronze skin, a lean muscular frame with broad shoulders and a narrow waist that tapered into the nicest ass she'd ever seen, rounded out what could only be described as a perfect living example of God's gift to women. The man personified satin and silk, fire and ice, sex and sensuality, and the wine and candlelight she so wantonly desired. All told, he was a damn fine white man.

It was a well-known fact Mr. Broussard was a highly sought-after, bona fide, honest-to-God ladies' man. His handsomeness would lend credence to such a claim, but it wasn't his looks alone that turned women's heads. There was something else about the man that could set a woman's senses on fire. He had a scent like no other, an actual natural scent that wafted into the air and drove women to nearly stampede like a herd of cattle.

The man's scent was to women like catnip was to cats—overpowering and irresistible. He could have any woman he wanted, and unfortunately, Sarona was no more immune to the natural power he wielded than any other member of the female sex. Knowing she was as susceptible as all the others, she did everything she could to stay off his radar and out of sight, but for some reason she couldn't fathom, every time she turned around, there he was.

The two of them had crossed paths off and on over the last year at venues like this, but had rarely engaged in what could be considered real conversation. They'd exchanged friendly flirtatious bantering, she teasing him about his reputation, he inviting her to explore the truth or myth of it for herself, but nothing more. She knew it was all just talk between them. She had no real concern he was actually interested in her, considering the obvious. She was black. She didn't fit his preferable parameters of attraction with her brown skin, full lips, big bust, and large, rounded bottom, all packaged in a daunting five-foot ten-inch frame. She was certain she had far too many curves for his taste. He'd once commented on her height and size and referred to her as an Amazon Queen. She silently chuckled, remembering the words they'd exchanged.

"That's right; I'm a *real* woman, so I suggest you save those Disneyland tactics you use for those anorexic, skin and bone-thin women you seem so fond of. If you step to me, you'd better bring it from the Wild Kingdom."

His eyes had grown wide with obvious surprise before he burst into a loud, boisterous laugh. She joined in, relieved that for once her habit of speaking first and thinking later hadn't landed her in hot water. Once the laughter died, he'd given her a curious look and responded in a much too intimate voice. "You know, Sarona, I'd be more than happy to go on safari with you any time. Just say the word."

She'd ignored his hint of implied interest because, for all her talk and bravado, there was no way in hell she was following him down that path. She'd told herself if there was any real interest, it was probably to satisfy the usual white man/black woman curiosity, and she'd be damned if she'd be seduced for the sake of curiosity. She'd seen and heard enough with her own eyes and ears to know any woman with half a brain and an ounce of self-preservation would steer clear of a man like him. She had no intention of getting mixed up in the games he liked to play.

She'd been around long enough to know that was all sex was to David—simply a game of stalk, capture, and conquer. "But damn." She sighed. "It sure is tempting to play."

She recognized the usual throng of women surrounding him, particularly the leader of the pack, Shelia Preston. Gossip had it David had recently dumped her after a brief fling, but the silly bitch didn't have sense enough to let go. Shelia mistakenly thought her good looks, fake boobs, and Daddy's money could get her any man she wanted. She thought material things entitled her to treat people with disrespect and allowed her the luxury of commanding the attention of any man, including David Broussard. Ordinarily that might have held true, but David Broussard wasn't just any man.

She had to admit, he was quite good at the hunt. Even now, while charming the women in front of him, he was scanning the room looking for his next target. By the look of determination on his face, he would have his next victim bagged and tagged in well under the five-day deadline. The man was lethal, and he looked every bit the predator he was.

She was *not* happy he was there, and her dismay at seeing him was testament to how she too was affected by his seductive persona. *God, the man's one big, walking pheromone,* she thought, disgusted with her irrepressible response to his presence.

In the mood for more Crimson Romance?
Check out *Together Again* by Peggy Bird
at CrimsonRomance.com.